THE LOUD HOUSE

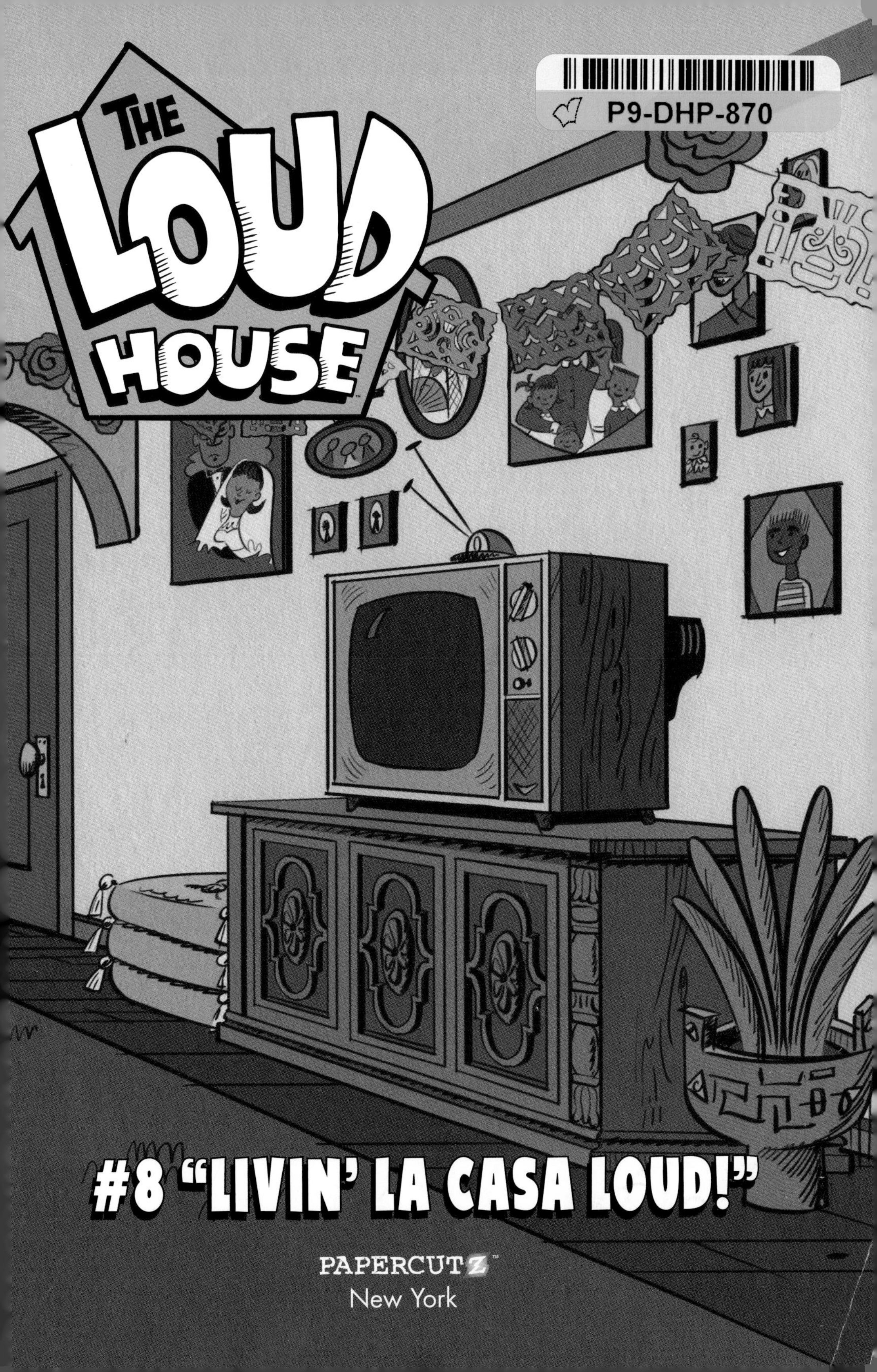

#8 "LIVIN' LA CASA LOUD!"

PAPERCUTZ
New York

nickelodeon GRAPHIC NOVELS AVAILABLE FROM PAPERCUTZ

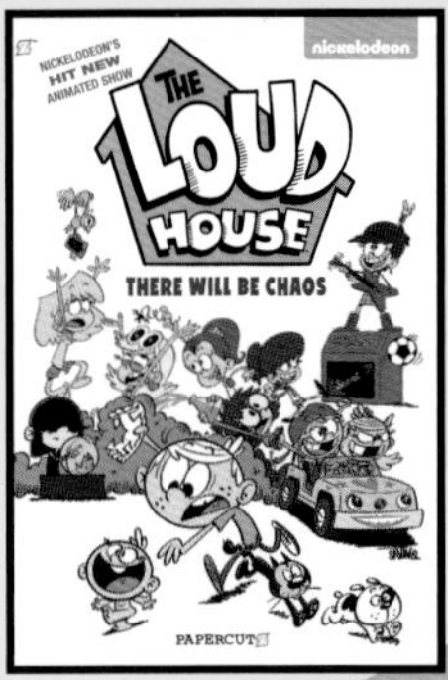
NICKELODEON'S HIT NEW ANIMATED SHOW
nickelodeon
THE LOUD HOUSE
THERE WILL BE CHAOS
PAPERCUTZ

THE LOUD HOUSE
#1
"There Will Be Chaos"

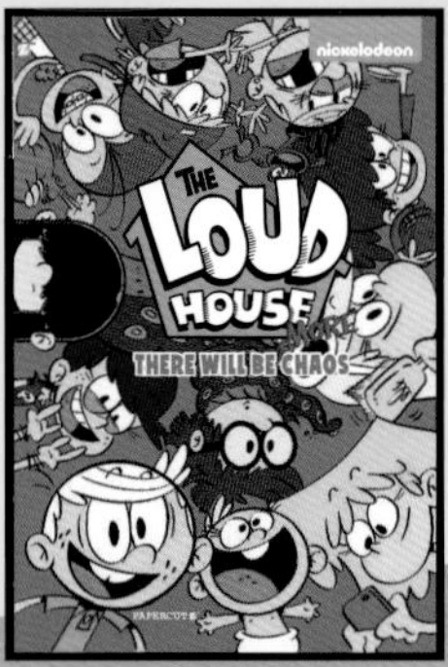
nickelodeon
THE LOUD HOUSE
THERE WILL BE CHAOS
PAPERCUTZ

THE LOUD HOUSE
#2
"There Will Be More Chaos"

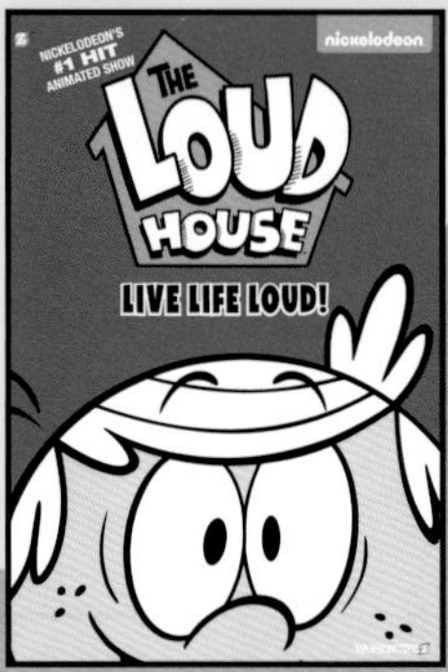
NICKELODEON'S #1 HIT ANIMATED SHOW
nickelodeon
THE LOUD HOUSE
LIVE LIFE LOUD!

THE LOUD HOUSE
#3
"Live Life Loud!"

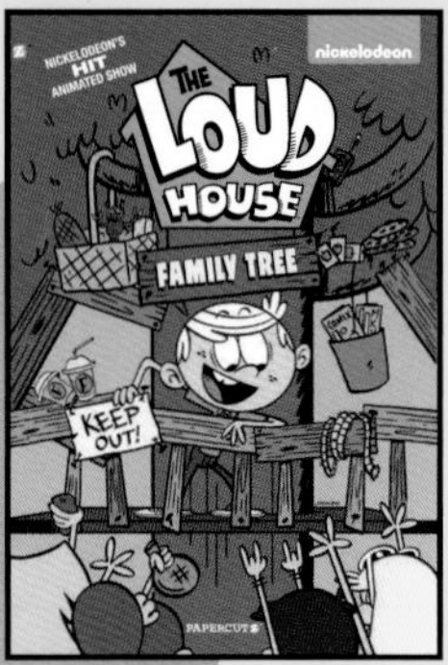
NICKELODEON'S HIT ANIMATED SHOW
nickelodeon
THE LOUD HOUSE
FAMILY TREE
KEEP OUT!
PAPERCUTZ

THE LOUD HOUSE
#4
"Family Tree"

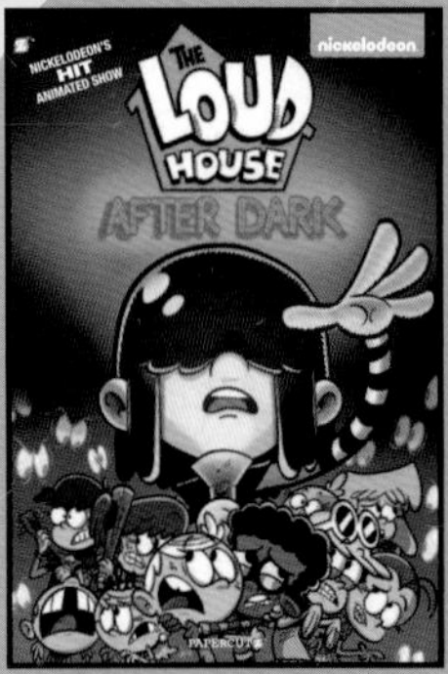
NICKELODEON'S HIT ANIMATED SHOW
nickelodeon
THE LOUD HOUSE
AFTER DARK
PAPERCUTZ

THE LOUD HOUSE
#5
"After Dark"

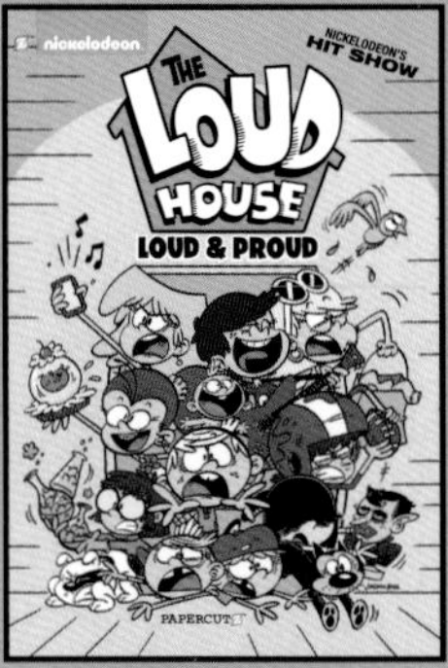
nickelodeon
NICKELODEON'S HIT SHOW
THE LOUD HOUSE
LOUD & PROUD
PAPERCUTZ

THE LOUD HOUSE
#6
"Loud and Proud"

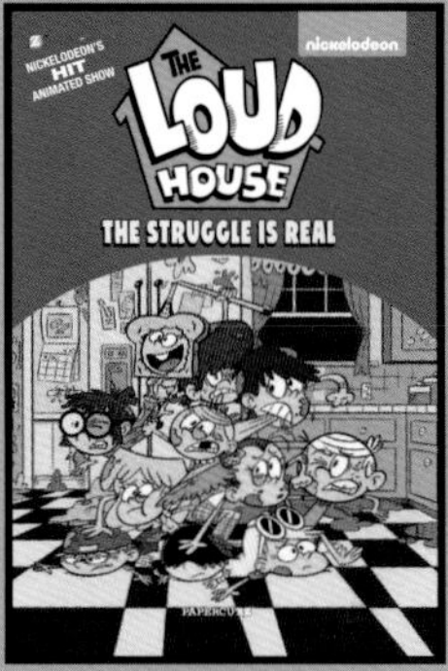
NICKELODEON'S HIT ANIMATED SHOW
nickelodeon
THE LOUD HOUSE
THE STRUGGLE IS REAL
PAPERCUTZ

THE LOUD HOUSE
#7
"The Struggle is Real"

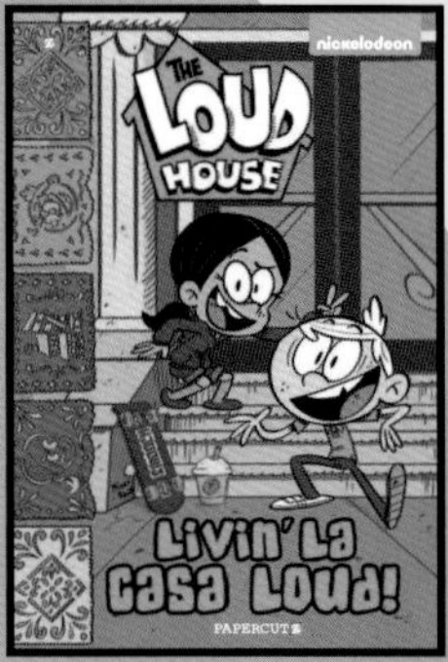
nickelodeon
THE LOUD HOUSE
Livin' La Casa Loud!
PAPERCUTZ

THE LOUD HOUSE
#8
"Livin' La Casa Loud"

COMING SOON

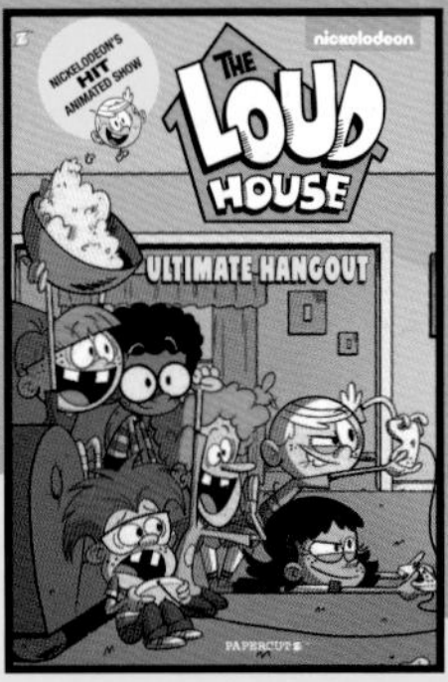
NICKELODEON'S HIT ANIMATED SHOW
nickelodeon
THE LOUD HOUSE
ULTIMATE HANGOUT
PAPERCUTZ

THE LOUD HOUSE
#9
"Ultimate Hangout"

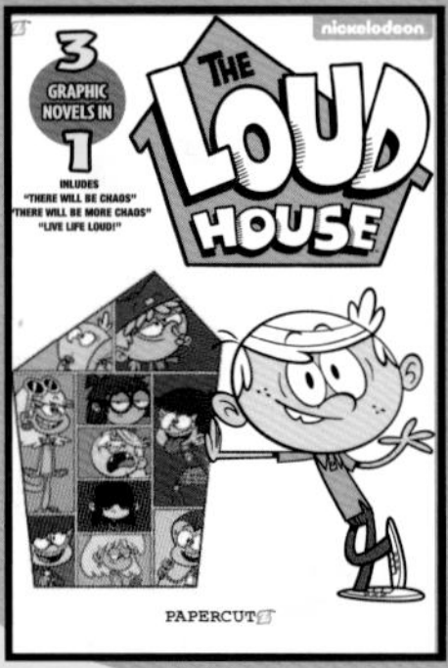
nickelodeon
3 GRAPHIC NOVELS IN 1
INCLUDES "THERE WILL BE CHAOS" "THERE WILL BE MORE CHAOS" "LIVE LIFE LOUD!"
THE LOUD HOUSE
PAPERCUTZ

THE LOUD HOUSE
3 IN 1
#1

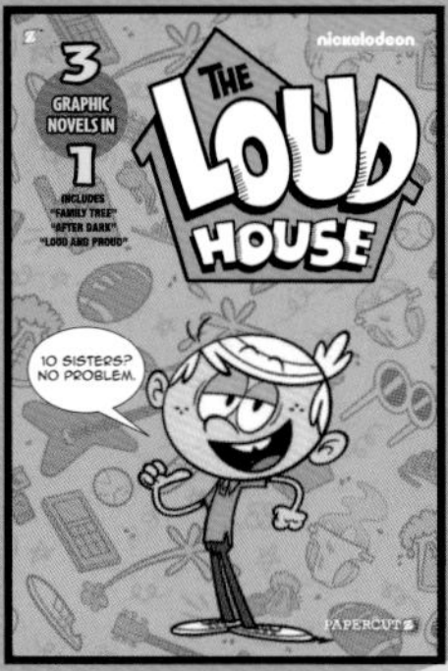
nickelodeon
3 GRAPHIC NOVELS IN 1
INCLUDES "FAMILY TREE" "AFTER DARK" "LOUD AND PROUD"
THE LOUD HOUSE
10 SISTERS? NO PROBLEM.
PAPERCUTZ

THE LOUD HOUSE
3 IN 1
#2

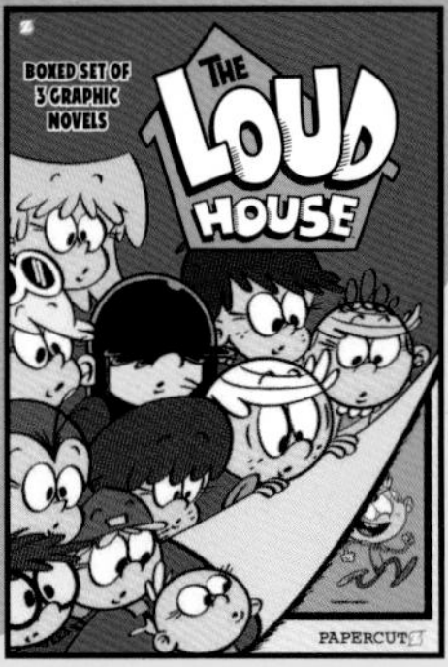
BOXED SET OF 3 GRAPHIC NOVELS
THE LOUD HOUSE
PAPERCUTZ

THE LOUD HOUSE
BOXED SET
$23.99

LOUD HOUSE graphic novels are available for $7.99 each in paperback, $12.99 each in hardcover. THE LOUD HOUSE 3 IN 1 collections are $14.99 each, in paperback only. THE LOUD HOUSE BOXED SET is available for $23.99. Available from booksellers everywhere. You can also order online from Papercutz.com, or call 1-800-886-1223, Monday through Friday, 9-5 EST. MC, Visa, and AmEx accepted.
To order by mail, please add $5.00 for postage and handling for the first book ordered, $1.00 for each additional book and make check payable to NBM Publishing.
Send to: Papercutz, 160 Broadway, Suite 700, East Wing, New York, NY 10038.

Nickelodeon graphic novels are also available digitally wherever e-books are sold.

THE LOUD HOUSE

#8 "LIVIN' LA CASA LOUD!"

nickelodeon THE LOUD HOUSE #8 "LIVIN' LA CASA LOUD!"

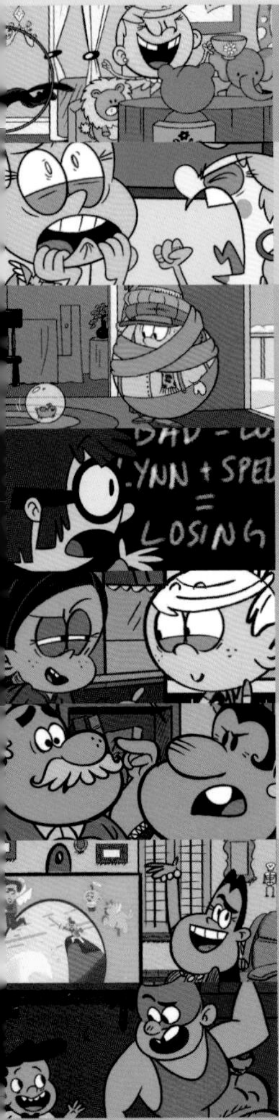

"LITTLE BIG TOP"
Ronda Pattison — Writer, Artist, Colorist
Wilson Ramos Jr. — Letterer

"FASHION VICTIM"
Hannah Watanabe-Rocco — Writer
Angela Zhang — Artist, Colorist
Wilson Ramos Jr. — Letterer

"SNOWBALL-ED!"
Ronda Pattison — Writer, Artist, Colorist
Wilson Ramos Jr. — Letterer

"STUDY BUDDIES"
Hannah Watanabe-Rocco — Writer
Angela Zhang — Artist, Colorist
Wilson Ramos Jr. — Letterer

"CITY TRICKERS"
Andrew Brooks — Writer
Gizelle Orbino — Artist, Colorist
Wilson Ramos Jr. — Letterer

"GOSSIP GUY"
Derek Fridolfs — Writer
Melissa Kleynowski —Penciler
Zazo Aguiar — Inker, Colorist
Wilson Ramos Jr. — Letterer

"LIFE IMITATES ART"
Angela Entzminger — Writer
Ivy Jordan — Artist, Colorist
Wilson Ramos Jr. — Letterer

"THE MASKED MAN"
Derek Fridolfs — Writer
Ivy Jordan — Artist, Colorist
Wilson Ramos Jr. — Letterer

"HIDE AND SNEAK"
Derek Fridolfs — Writer
Daniela Rodriguez — Artist, Colorist
Wilson Ramos Jr. — Letterer

"FEEDING FRENZY"
Brian Smith — Writer
Isaiah Kim — Artist
Ronda Pattison — Colorist
Wilson Ramos Jr. — Letterer

"SUPER HANGOUT TIME ACTIVATE"
Hannah Watanabe-Rocco — Writer
Chris Sabatino — Artist, Colorist
Wilson Ramos Jr. — Letterer

"RAIN, RAIN, HERE TO STAY"
Andrew Brooks — Writer
Erin Hyde — Artist, Colorist
Wilson Ramos Jr. — Letterer

"PARTY ANIMALS"
Derek Fridolfs — Writer
Chris Sabatino — Artist
Zazo Aguiar — Colorist
Wilson Ramos Jr. — Letterer

"WASHED UP"
Derek Fridolfs — Writer
Kelsey Wooley — Artist, Colorist
Wilson Ramos Jr. — Letterer

"THE GREAT ESCAPE"
Derek Fridolfs — Writer
Suzannah Rowntree — Penciler
Zazo Aguiar — Inker, Colorist
Wilson Ramos Jr. — Letterer

"MY BOBBY AND ME"
Angela Entzminger — Writer
Way Singleton — Artist, Colorist
Wilson Ramos Jr. — Letterer

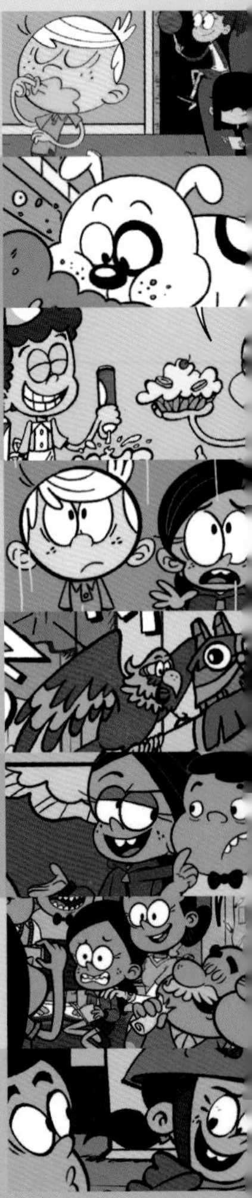

MIGUEL PUGA — Cover Artist
JORDAN ROSATO — Endpapers
JAMES SALERNO — Sr. Art Director/Nickelodeon
JAYJAY JACKSON — Design
PRINCESS BIZARES, CARLO PADILLA, SEAN GANTKA, ANGELA ENTZMINGER, DANA CLUVERIUS, MOLLIE FREILICH — Special Thanks
JEFF WHITMAN — Editor
IZZY BOYCE-BLANCHARD — Editorial Intern
JOAN HILTY — Editor/Nickelodeon
JIM SALICRUP
EDITOR-IN-CHIEF

ISBN: 978-1-5458-0343-1 paperback edition
ISBN: 978-1-5458-0342-4 hardcover edition

www.papercutz.com

Papercutz books may be purchased for business or promotional use. For information on bulk purchases please contact Macmillan Corporate and Premium Sales Department at (800) 221-7945 x5442.

Printed in China
November 2019

Distributed by Macmillan
First Printing

MEET THE LOUD FAMILY and friends!

LINCOLN LOUD
THE MIDDLE CHILD (11)

At 11 years old, Lincoln is the middle child, with five older sisters and five younger sisters. He has learned that surviving the Loud household means staying a step ahead. He's the man with a plan, always coming up with a way to get what he wants or deal with a problem, even if things inevitably go wrong. Being the only boy comes with some perks. Lincoln gets his own room – even if it's just a converted linen closet. On the other hand, being the only boy also means he sometimes gets a little too much attention from his sisters. They mother him, tease him, and use him as the occasional lab rat or fashion show participant. Lincoln's sisters may drive him crazy, but he loves them and is always willing to help out if they need him.

LORI LOUD
THE OLDEST (17)

As the first-born child of the Loud Clan, Lori sees herself as the boss of all her siblings. She feels she's paved the way for them and deserves extra respect. Her signature traits are rolling her eyes, texting her boyfriend, Bobby, and literally saying "literally" all the time. Because she's the oldest and most experienced sibling, Lori can be a great ally, so it pays to stay on her good side, especially since she can drive.

LENI LOUD
THE FASHIONISTA (16)

Leni spends most of her time designing outfits and accessorizing. She always falls for Luan's pranks, and sometimes walks into walls when she's talking (she's not great at doing two things at once). Leni might be flighty, but she's the sweetest of the Loud siblings and truly has a heart of gold (even though she's pretty sure it's a heart of blood).

LUNA LOUD
THE ROCK STAR (15)

Luna is loud, boisterous and freewheeling, and her energy is always cranked to 11. She thinks about music so much that she even talks in song lyrics. On the off-chance she doesn't have her guitar with her, everything can and will be turned into a musical instrument. You can always count on Luna to help out, and she'll do most anything you ask, as long as you're okay with her supplying a rocking guitar accompaniment.

LYNN LOUD
THE ATHLETE (13)

Lynn is athletic and full of energy and is always looking for a teammate. With her, it's all sports all the time. She'll turn anything into a sport. Putting away eggs? Jump shot! Score! Cleaning up the eggs? Slap shot! Score! Lynn is very competitive, but despite her competitive nature, she always tries to just have a good time.

MR. COCONUTS

Luan Loud's wise-cracking dummy.

LUAN LOUD
THE JOKESTER (14)

Luan's a standup comedienne who provides a nonstop barrage of silly puns. She's big on prop comedy too – squirting flowers and whoopee cushions – so you have to be on your toes whenever she's around. She loves to pull pranks and is a really good ventriloquist – she is often found doing bits with her dummy, Mr. Coconuts. Luan never lets anything get her down; to her, laughter IS the best medicine.

EL DIABLO

LOLA LOUD
THE BEAUTY QUEEN (6)

Lola could not be more different from her twin sister, Lana. She's a pageant powerhouse whose interests include glitter, photo shoots, and her own beautiful, beautiful face. But don't let her cute, gap-toothed smile fool you; underneath all the sugar and spice lurks a Machiavellian mastermind. Whatever Lola wants, Lola gets – or else. She's the eyes and ears of the household and never resists an opportunity to tattle on troublemakers. But if you stay on Lola's good side, you've got yourself a fierce ally – and a lifetime supply of free makeovers.

LUCY LOUD
THE EMO (8)

You can always count on Lucy to give the morbid point of view in any given situation. She is obsessed with all things spooky and dark – funerals, vampires, séances, and the like. She wears mostly black and writes moody poetry. She's usually quiet and keeps to herself. Lucy has a way of mysteriously appearing out of nowhere, and try as they might, her siblings never get used to this.

LANA LOUD
THE TOMBOY (6)

Lana is the rough-and-tumble sparkplug counterpart to her twin sister, Lola. She's all about reptiles, mud pies, and muffler repair. She's the resident Ms. Fix-it and is always ready to lend a hand – the dirtier the job, the better. Need your toilet unclogged? Snake fed? Back-zit popped? Lana's your gal. All she asks in return is a little A-B-C gum, or a handful of kibble (she often sneaks it from the dog bowl).

FANGS

HOPS

WALT

CLIFF

LISA LOUD
THE GENIUS (4)

Lisa is smarter than the rest of her siblings combined. She'll most likely be a rocket scientist, or a brain surgeon, or an evil genius who takes over the world. Lisa spends most of her time working in her lab (the family has gotten used to the explosions), and says her research leaves little time for frivolous human pursuits like "playing" or "getting haircuts." That said, she's always there to help with a homework question, or to explain why the sky is blue, or to point out the structural flaws in someone's pillow fort. Lisa says it's the least she can do for her favorite test subjects, er, siblings.

LILY LOUD
THE BABY (15 MONTHS)

Lily is a giggly, drooly, diaper-ditching free spirit, affectionately known as "the poop machine." You can't keep a nappy on this kid – she's like a teething Houdini. But even when Lily's running wild, dropping rancid diaper bombs, or drooling all over the remote, she always brings a smile to everyone's face (and a clothespin to their nose). Lily is everyone's favorite little buddy, and the whole family loves her unconditionally.

CHARLES

BITEY

GEO

RITA LOUD

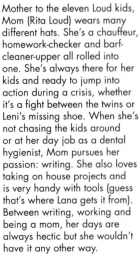

Mother to the eleven Loud kids, Mom (Rita Loud) wears many different hats. She's a chauffeur, homework-checker and barf-cleaner-upper all rolled into one. She's always there for her kids and ready to jump into action during a crisis, whether it's a fight between the twins or Leni's missing shoe. When she's not chasing the kids around or at her day job as a dental hygienist, Mom pursues her passion: writing. She also loves taking on house projects and is very handy with tools (guess that's where Lana gets it from). Between writing, working and being a mom, her days are always hectic but she wouldn't have it any other way.

LYNN LOUD SR.

Dad (Lynn Loud Sr.) is a fun-loving, upbeat aspiring chef. A kid-at-heart, he's not above taking part in the kids' zany schemes. In addition to cooking, Dad loves his van, playing the cowbell and making puns. Before meeting Mom, Dad spent a semester in England and has been obsessed with British culture ever since – and sometimes "accidentally" slips into a British accent. When Dad's not wrangling the kids, he's pursuing his dream of opening his own restaurant where he hopes to make his "Lynn-sagnas" world-famous.

RONNIE ANNE SANTIAGO

Ronnie Anne's an independent spirit who's into skating, gaming and pranking. Strong-willed and a little gruff, she isn't into excessive displays of emotion. But don't be fooled – she has a sweet side, too, fostered by years of taking care of her mother and brother. And though her new extended family can be a little overwhelming, she appreciates how loving, caring, and fun they can be.

BOBBY SANTIAGO

Ronnie Anne's older brother, Bobby is a sweet, responsible, loyal high-school senior who works in the family's bodega. Bobby is very devoted to his family. He's Grandpa's right hand man and can't wait to one day take over the bodega for him. Bobby's a big kid and a bit of a klutz, which sometimes gets him into pickles, like locking himself in the freezer case. But he makes up for any work mishaps with his great customer skills – everyone in the neighborhood loves him.

MARIA CASAGRANDE SANTIAGO

She's the mother of Bobby and Ronnie Anne. A hardworking nurse, she doesn't get to spend a lot of time with her kids, but when she does she treasures it. Maria is calm and rational but often worries about whether she's doing enough for her kids. Maria, Bobby, and Ronnie Anne are a close-knit trio who were used to having only each other – until they moved in with their extended family.

HECTOR CASAGRANDE

He's the father of Carlos and Maria and the grandfather of six. The patriarch of the Casagrande Family, Hector wears the pants in the family (or at least thinks he does). He is the owner of the bodega on the ground floor of their apartment building and takes great pride in his work, his family, and being the unofficial "mayor" of the block. He's charismatic, friendly, and also a huge gossip (although he tries to deny it).

ROSA CASAGRANDE

She's the mother of Carlos and Maria and wife to Hector. Rosa is a gifted cook and has a sixth sense about knowing when anyone in her house is hungry. The wisest of the bunch, Rosa is really the head of the household but lets Hector think he is. She's spiritual and often tries to fix problems or illnesses with home remedies or potions. She's protective of all her family and at times can be a bit smothering.

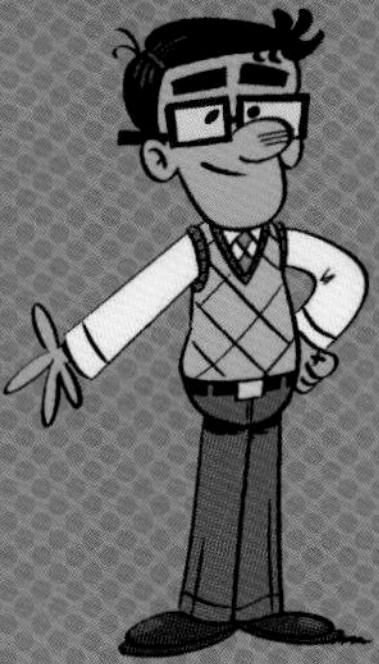

CARLOS CASAGRANDE

He's the father of four kids (Carlota, CJ, Carl, and Carlitos), husband of Frida, and brother of Maria. He's a professor of marine biology at a local college and always has his head in a book. He's a pretty easygoing guy compared to his sometimes overly emotional relatives. Carlos is pragmatic, a caring father, and loves to rattle off useless tidbits of information.

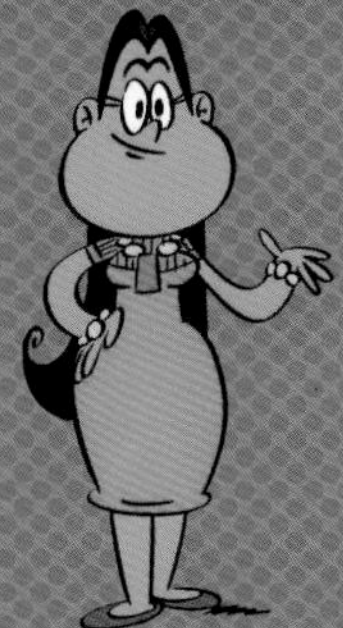

FRIDA PUGA CASAGRANDE

She's the mother to Carlota, CJ, Carl, and Carlitos and wife to Carlos. She's an artist-type, always taking photos of the family. She tends to cry when she's overcome with sadness, anger, happiness... basically, she cries a lot. She's excitable, game for fun, passionate, and loves her family more than anything. All she ever wants is for her entire family to be in the same room. But when that happens, all she can do is cry and take photos.

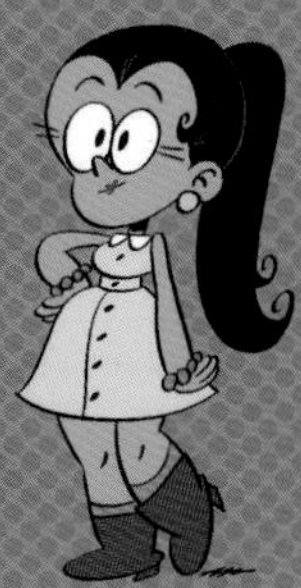

CARLOTA CASAGRANDE

The oldest child of Carlos and Frida. She's social, fun-loving, and desperately wants to be the big sister to Ronnie Anne. Carlota has a very distinctive vintage style, which she tries to share with Ronnie Anne, who couldn't be less interested.

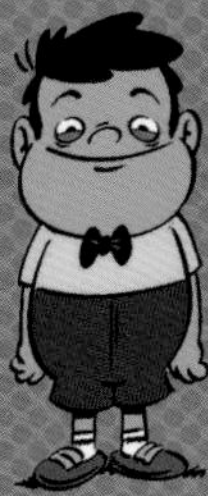

CJ (CARLOS JR.) CASAGRANDE

CJ was born with Down syndrome. He's the sunshine in everyone's life and always wants to play. He will often lighten the mood of a tense situation with his honest remarks. He adores Bobby and always wants to be around him (which is A-OK with Bobby, who sees CJ as a little brother). CJ asks to wear a bowtie every day no matter the occasion and is hardly ever without a smile on his face. He's definitely a glass-half-full kind of guy.

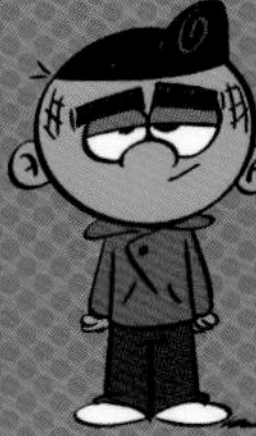

CARL CASAGRANDE

Carl is 6 going on 30. He thinks of himself as a suave, romantic ladies' man. He's confident and outgoing. When he sees something he likes, he goes for it (even if it's Bobby's girlfriend, Lori). He cares about his appearance even more than Carlota and often uses her hair products (much to her chagrin). He hates to be reminded that he's only six and is emasculated whenever someone notices him snuggling his blankie or sucking his thumb. Carl is convinced that Bobby is his biggest rival and is always trying to beat Bobby (which Bobby is unaware of).

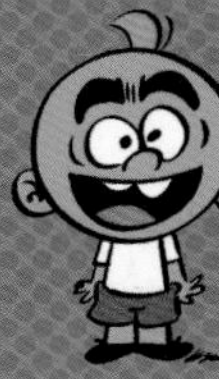

CARLITOS CASAGRANDE

The redheaded toddler who is always mimicking everyone's behavior, even the dog's. He's playful, rambunctious, and loves to play with the family pets.

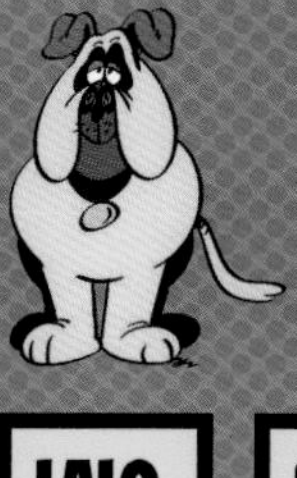

LALO

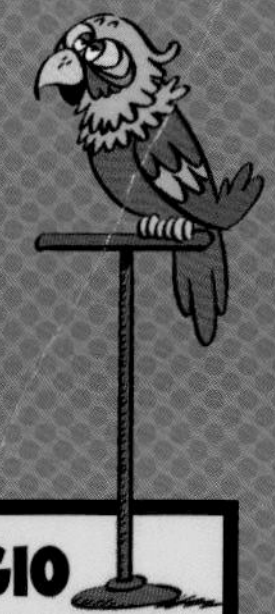

SERGIO

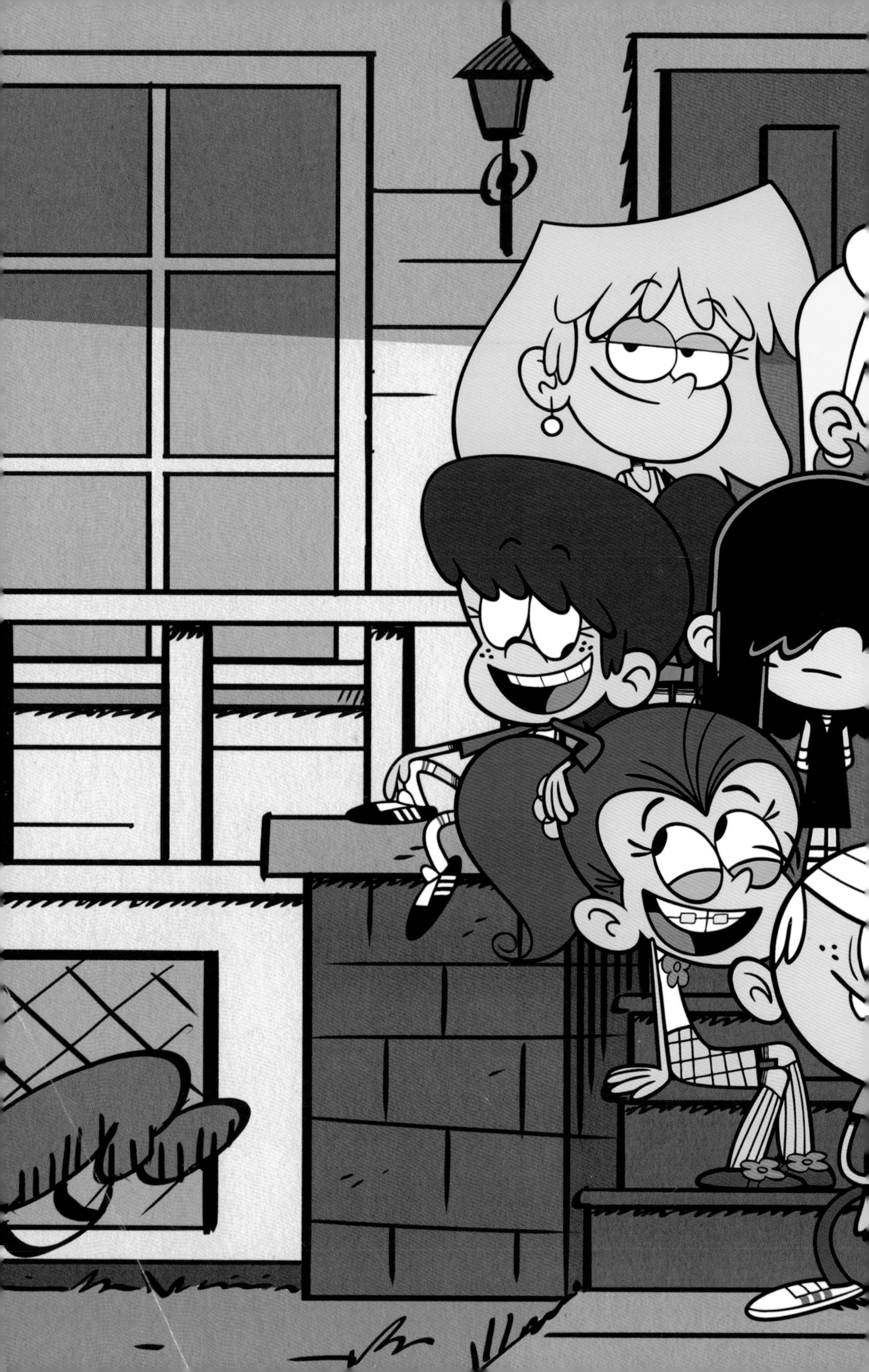

LIFE WITH THE LOUDS

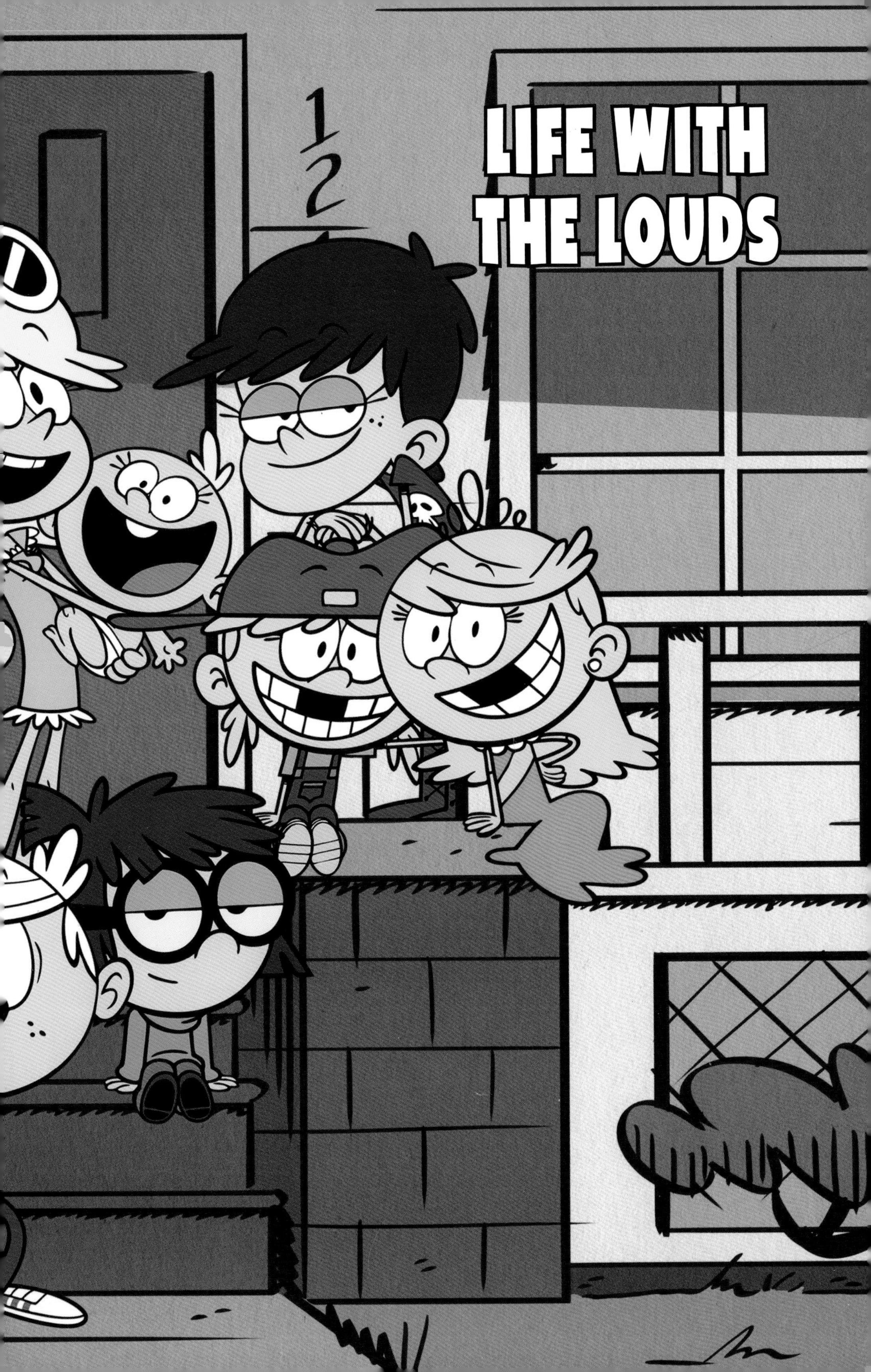

"LITTLE BIG TOP"

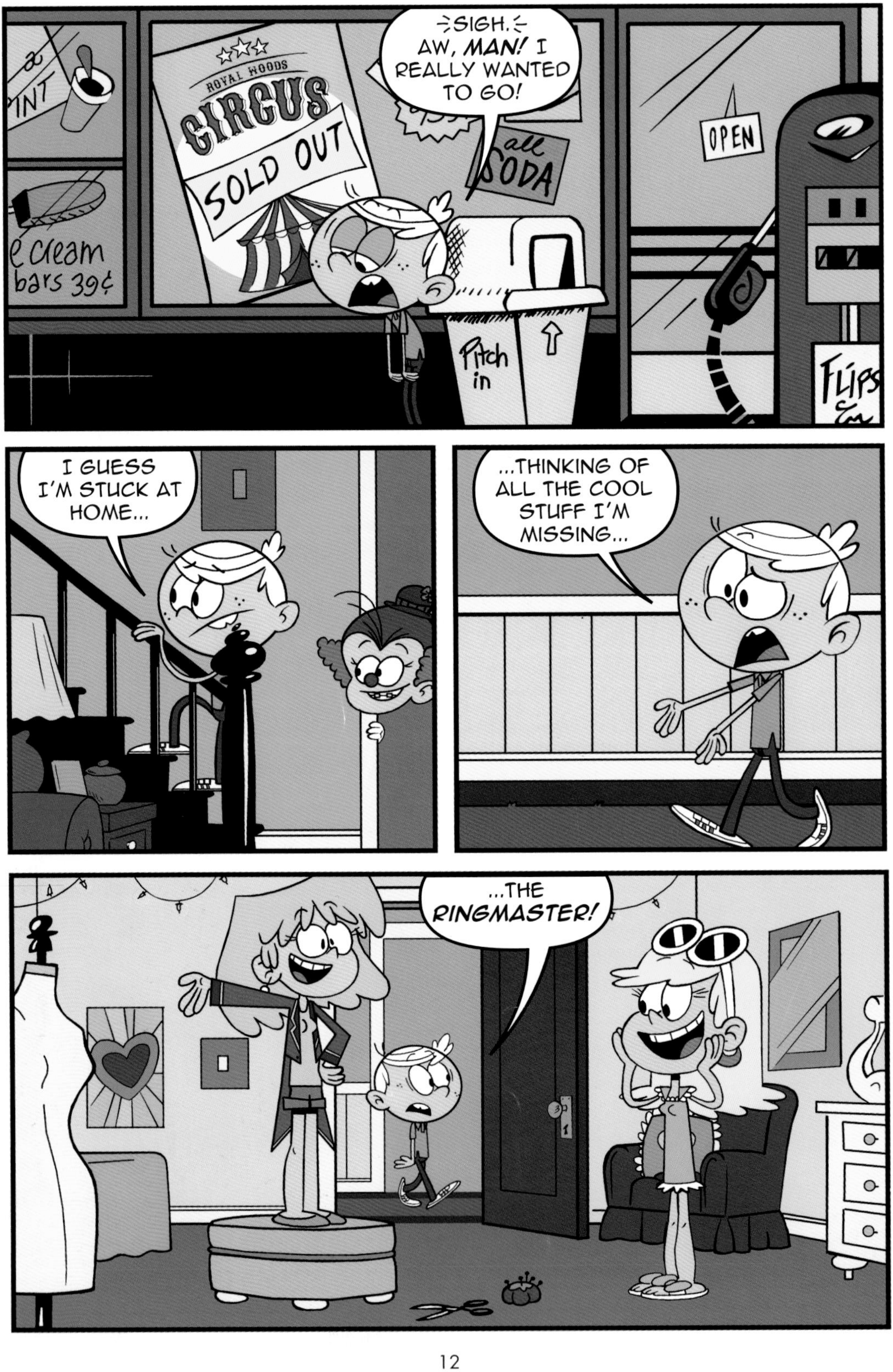
ROYAL WOODS
CIRCUS
SOLD OUT
all SODA
OPEN
e cream bars 39¢
Pitch in
SIGH. AW, *MAN!* I REALLY WANTED TO GO!
I GUESS I'M STUCK AT HOME...
...THINKING OF ALL THE COOL STUFF I'M MISSING...
...THE *RINGMASTER!*

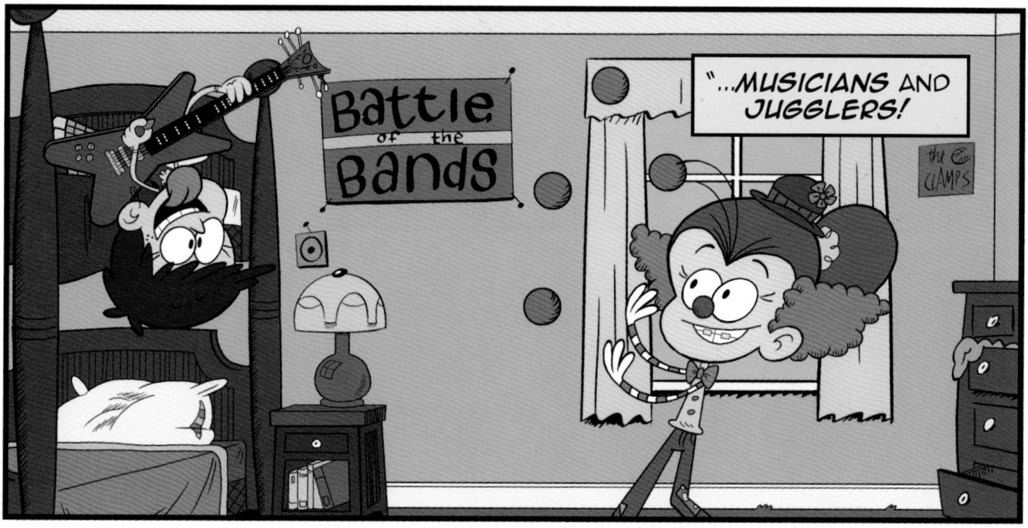
Battle of the Bands
"...MUSICIANS AND JUGGLERS!
the CLAMPS

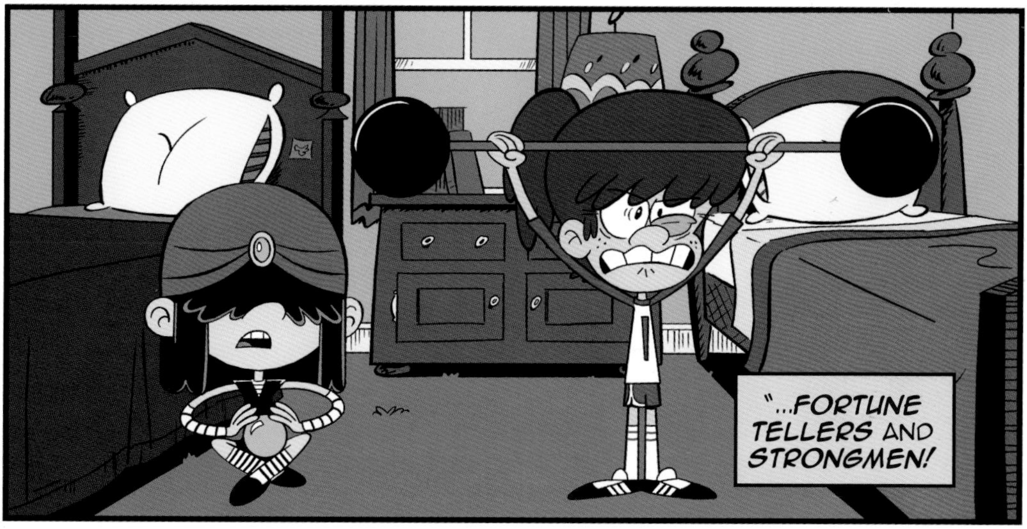
"...FORTUNE TELLERS AND STRONGMEN!

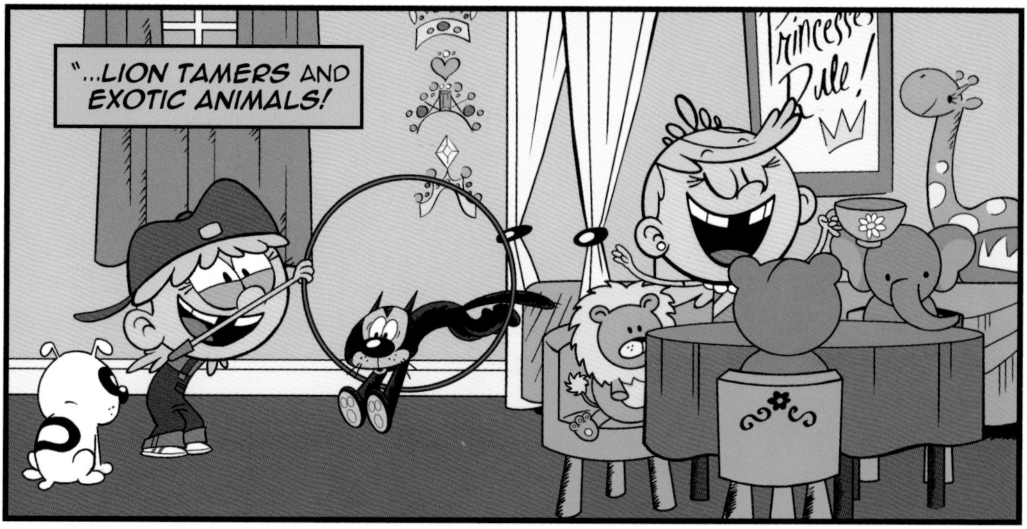
"...LION TAMERS AND EXOTIC ANIMALS!
Princesses Rule!

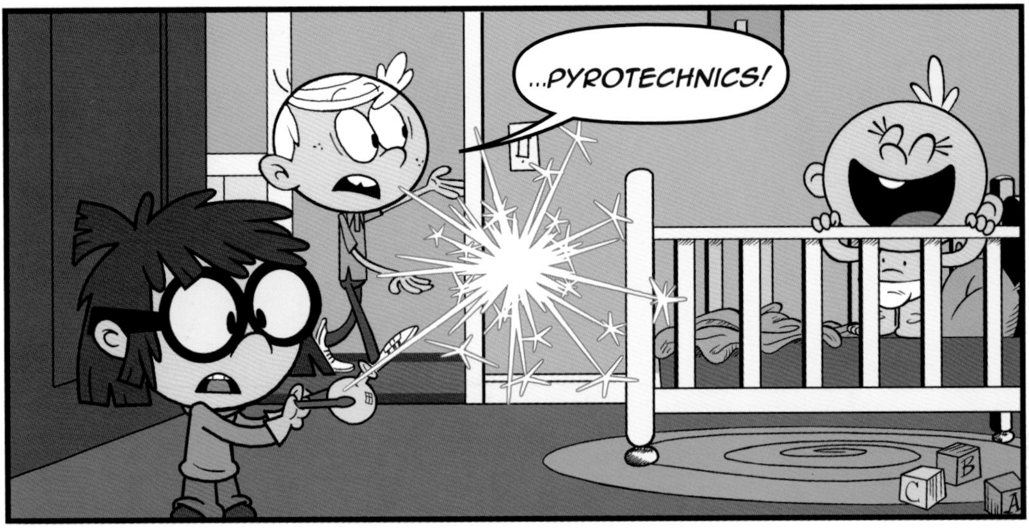
...PYROTECHNICS!

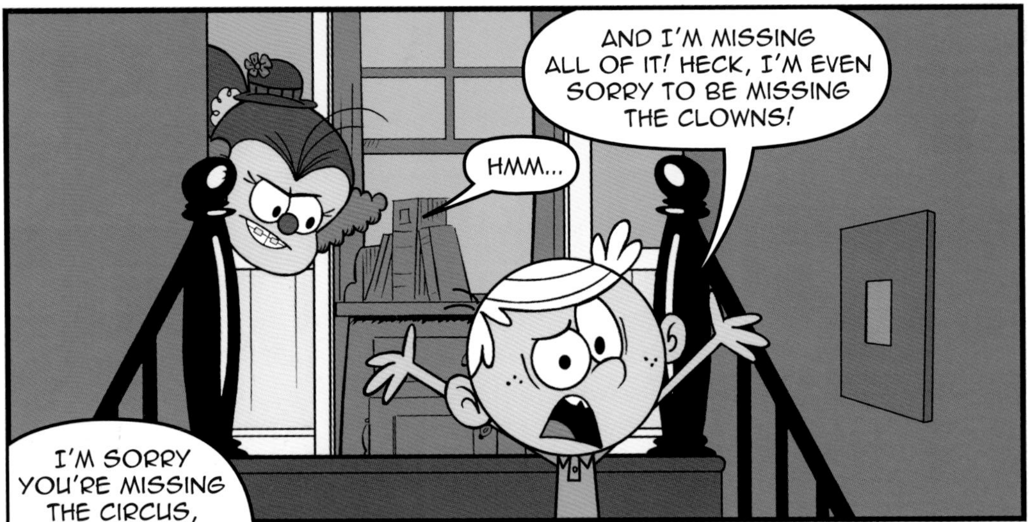
AND I'M MISSING ALL OF IT! HECK, I'M EVEN SORRY TO BE MISSING THE CLOWNS!
HMM...

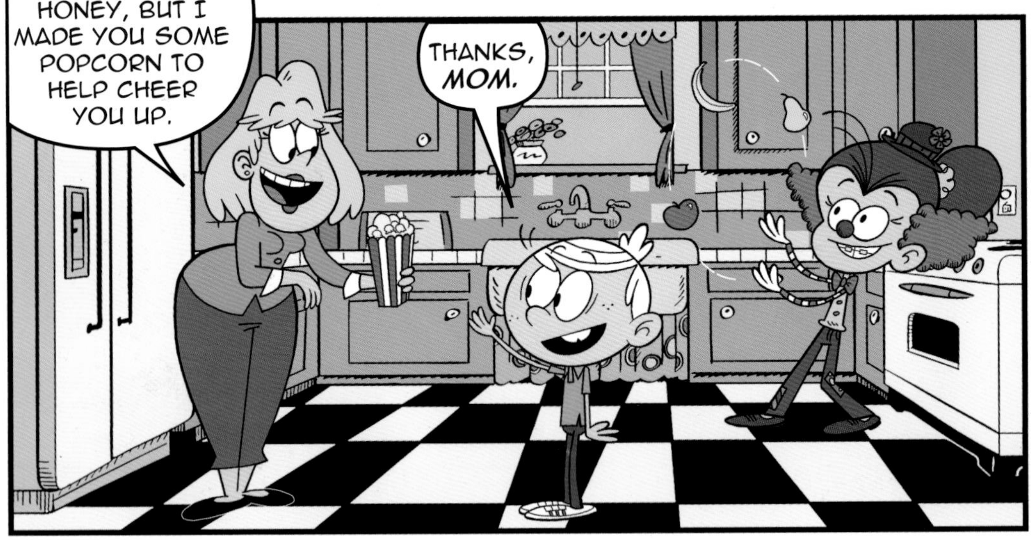
I'M SORRY YOU'RE MISSING THE CIRCUS, HONEY, BUT I MADE YOU SOME POPCORN TO HELP CHEER YOU UP.
THANKS, MOM.

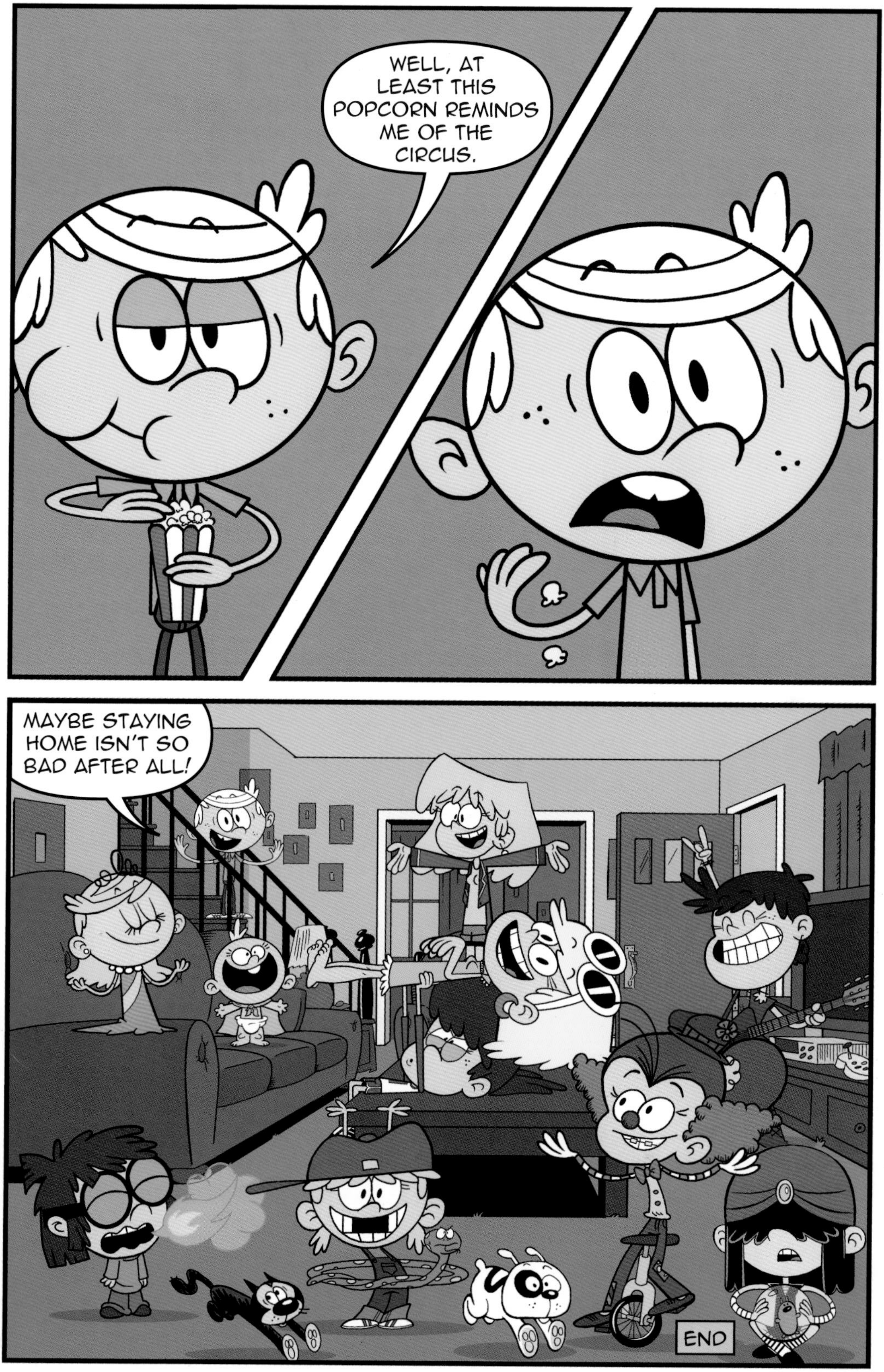
WELL, AT LEAST THIS POPCORN REMINDS ME OF THE CIRCUS.
MAYBE STAYING HOME ISN'T SO BAD AFTER ALL!
END

"HIDE AND SNEAK"

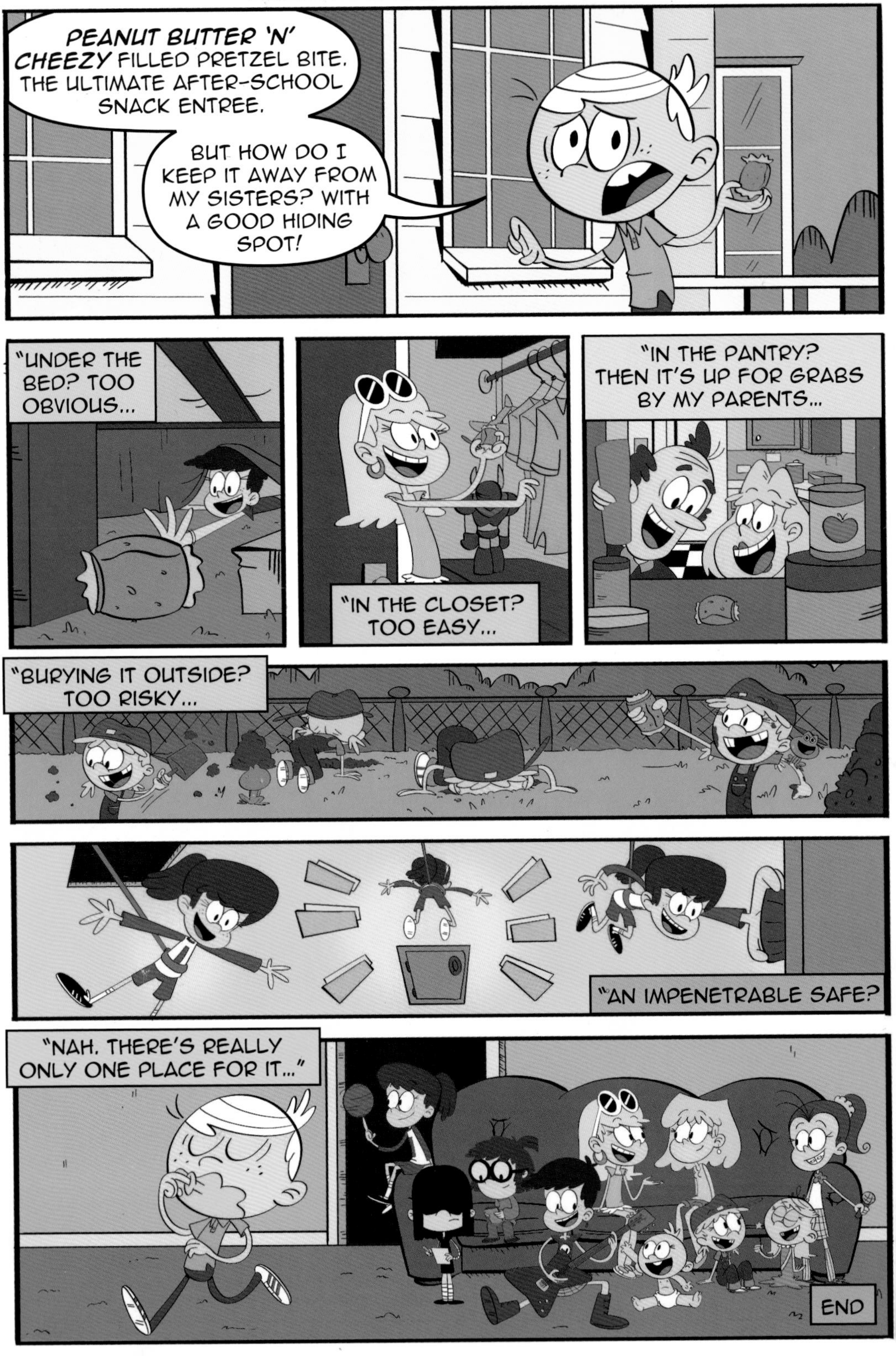

PEANUT BUTTER 'N' CHEEZY FILLED PRETZEL BITE. THE ULTIMATE AFTER-SCHOOL SNACK ENTREE.
BUT HOW DO I KEEP IT AWAY FROM MY SISTERS? WITH A GOOD HIDING SPOT!
"UNDER THE BED? TOO OBVIOUS...
"IN THE CLOSET? TOO EASY...
"IN THE PANTRY? THEN IT'S UP FOR GRABS BY MY PARENTS...
"BURYING IT OUTSIDE? TOO RISKY...
"AN IMPENETRABLE SAFE?
"NAH. THERE'S REALLY ONLY ONE PLACE FOR IT..."
END

"FASHION VICTIM"

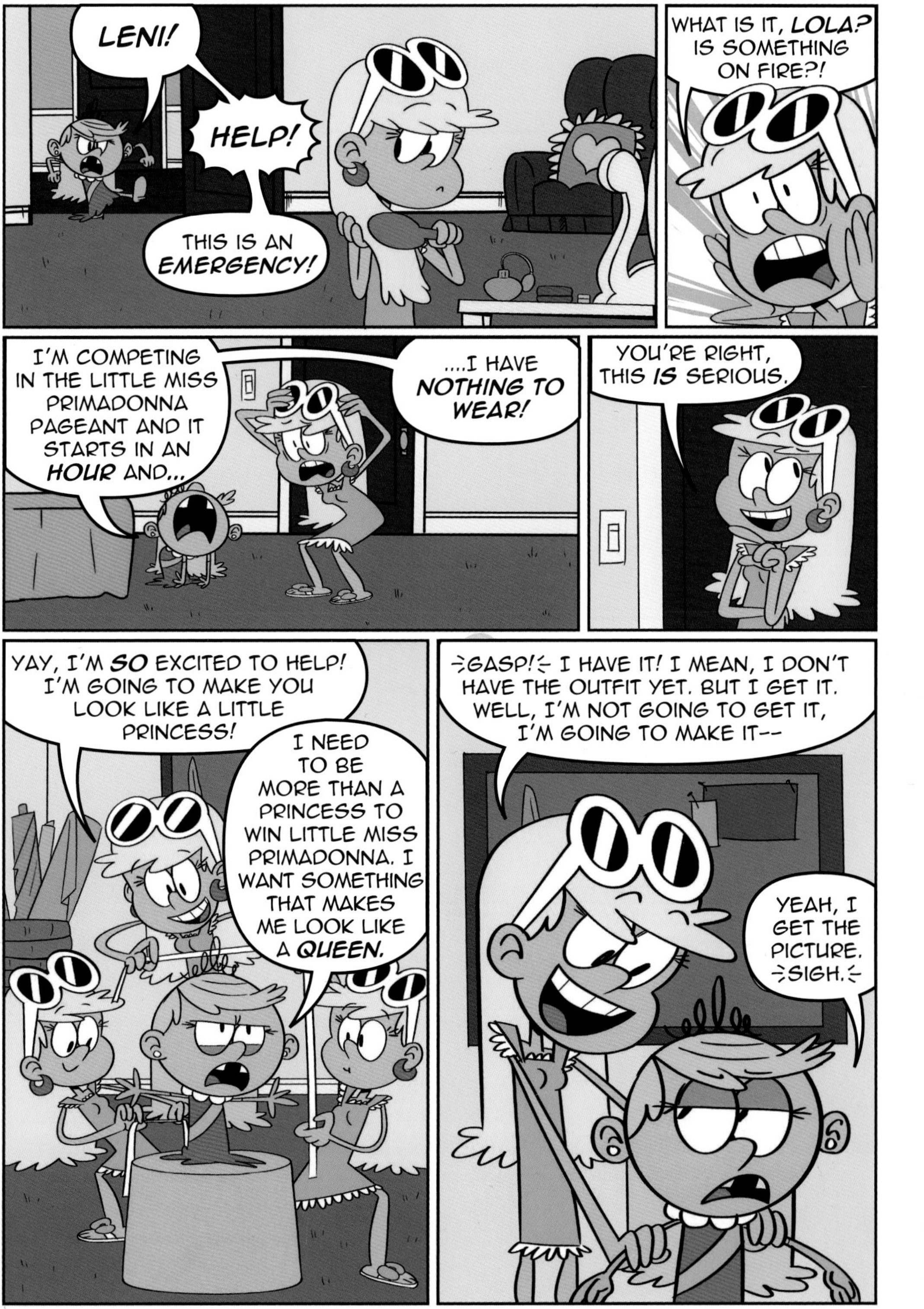

LENI!
HELP!
THIS IS AN EMERGENCY!
WHAT IS IT, LOLA? IS SOMETHING ON FIRE?!
I'M COMPETING IN THE LITTLE MISS PRIMADONNA PAGEANT AND IT STARTS IN AN HOUR AND...
....I HAVE NOTHING TO WEAR!
YOU'RE RIGHT, THIS IS SERIOUS.
YAY, I'M SO EXCITED TO HELP! I'M GOING TO MAKE YOU LOOK LIKE A LITTLE PRINCESS!
I NEED TO BE MORE THAN A PRINCESS TO WIN LITTLE MISS PRIMADONNA. I WANT SOMETHING THAT MAKES ME LOOK LIKE A QUEEN.
GASP! I HAVE IT! I MEAN, I DON'T HAVE THE OUTFIT YET. BUT I GET IT. WELL, I'M NOT GOING TO GET IT, I'M GOING TO MAKE IT--
YEAH, I GET THE PICTURE. SIGH.

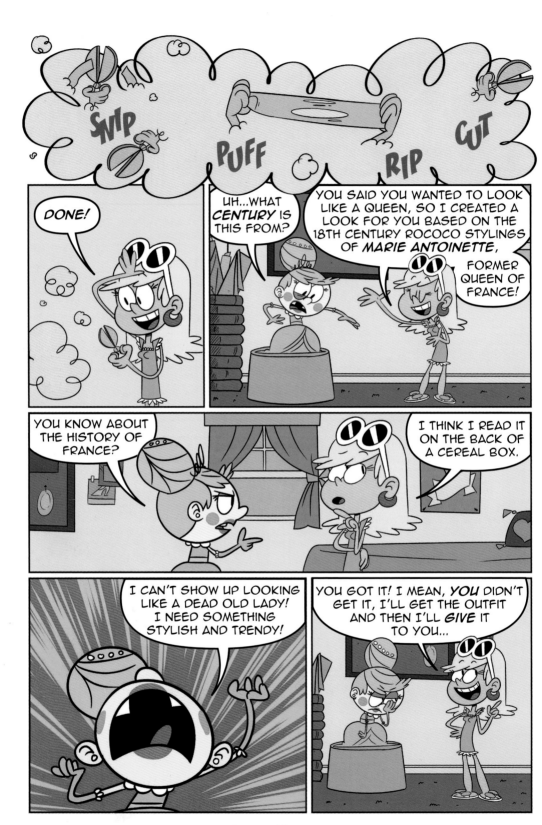

SNIP

PUFF

RIP

CUT

DONE!

UH...WHAT CENTURY IS THIS FROM?

YOU SAID YOU WANTED TO LOOK LIKE A QUEEN, SO I CREATED A LOOK FOR YOU BASED ON THE 18TH CENTURY ROCOCO STYLINGS OF *MARIE ANTOINETTE,* FORMER QUEEN OF FRANCE!

YOU KNOW ABOUT THE HISTORY OF FRANCE?

I THINK I READ IT ON THE BACK OF A CEREAL BOX.

I CAN'T SHOW UP LOOKING LIKE A DEAD OLD LADY! I NEED SOMETHING STYLISH AND TRENDY!

YOU GOT IT! I MEAN, *YOU* DIDN'T GET IT, I'LL GET THE OUTFIT AND THEN I'LL *GIVE* IT TO YOU...

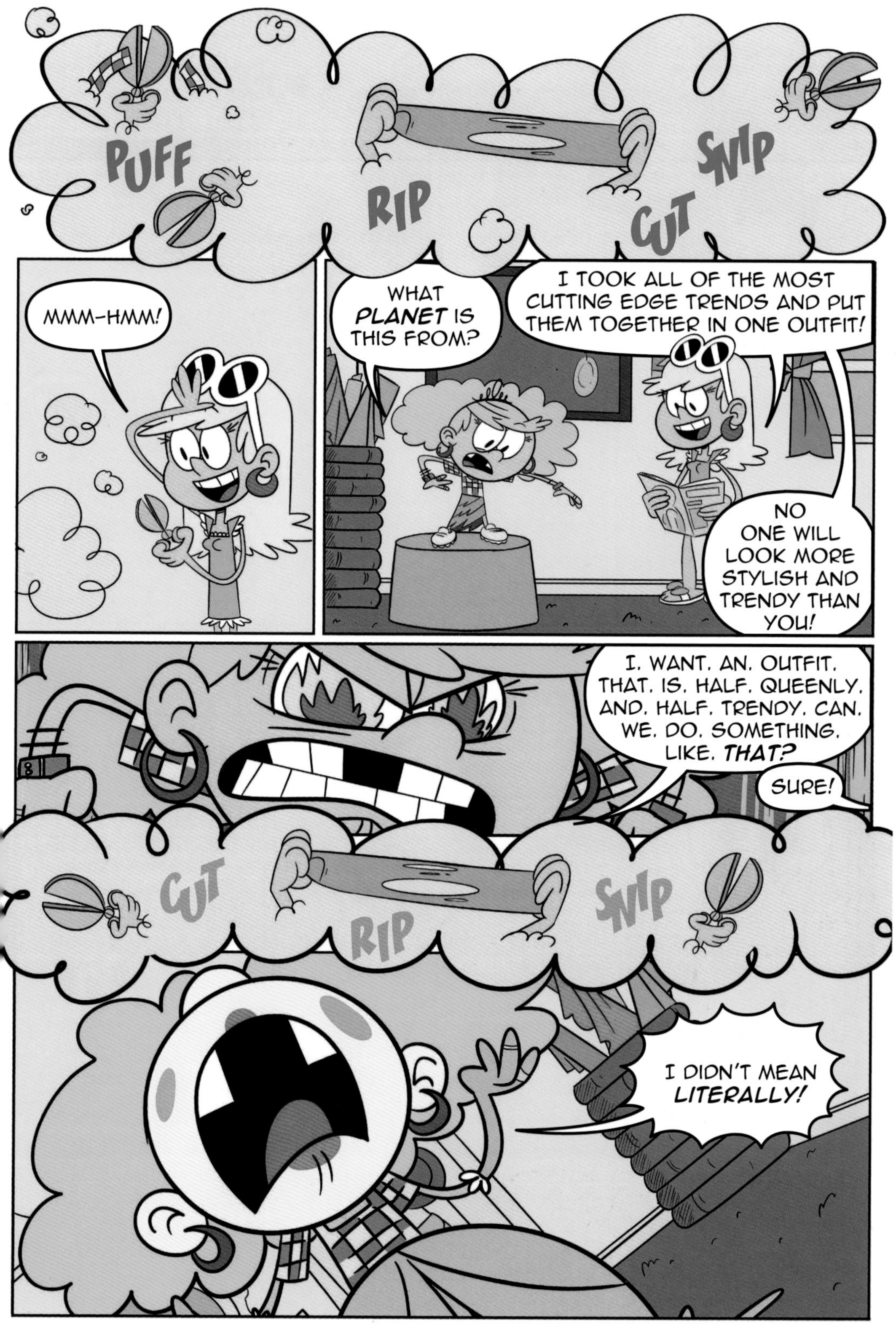
PUFF
RIP
CUT
SNIP
MMM-HMM!
WHAT *PLANET* IS THIS FROM?
I TOOK ALL OF THE MOST CUTTING EDGE TRENDS AND PUT THEM TOGETHER IN ONE OUTFIT!
NO ONE WILL LOOK MORE STYLISH AND TRENDY THAN YOU!
I. WANT. AN. OUTFIT. THAT. IS. HALF. QUEENLY. AND. HALF. TRENDY. CAN. WE. DO. SOMETHING. LIKE. *THAT?*
SURE!
CUT
RIP
SNIP
I DIDN'T MEAN *LITERALLY!*

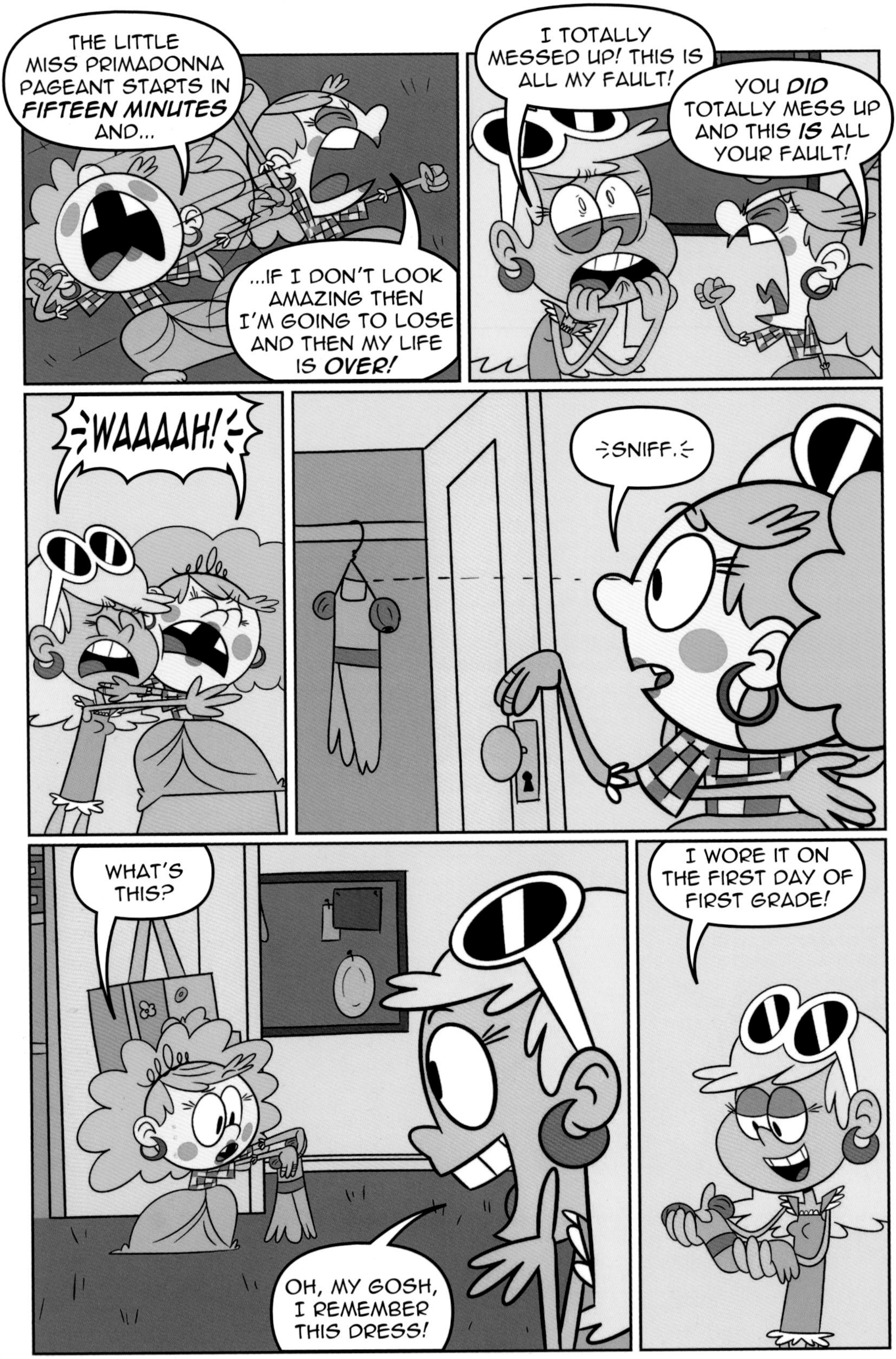
THE LITTLE MISS PRIMADONNA PAGEANT STARTS IN FIFTEEN MINUTES AND...
...IF I DON'T LOOK AMAZING THEN I'M GOING TO LOSE AND THEN MY LIFE IS OVER!
I TOTALLY MESSED UP! THIS IS ALL MY FAULT!
YOU DID TOTALLY MESS UP AND THIS IS ALL YOUR FAULT!
WAAAAH!
SNIFF.
WHAT'S THIS?
OH, MY GOSH, I REMEMBER THIS DRESS!
I WORE IT ON THE FIRST DAY OF FIRST GRADE!

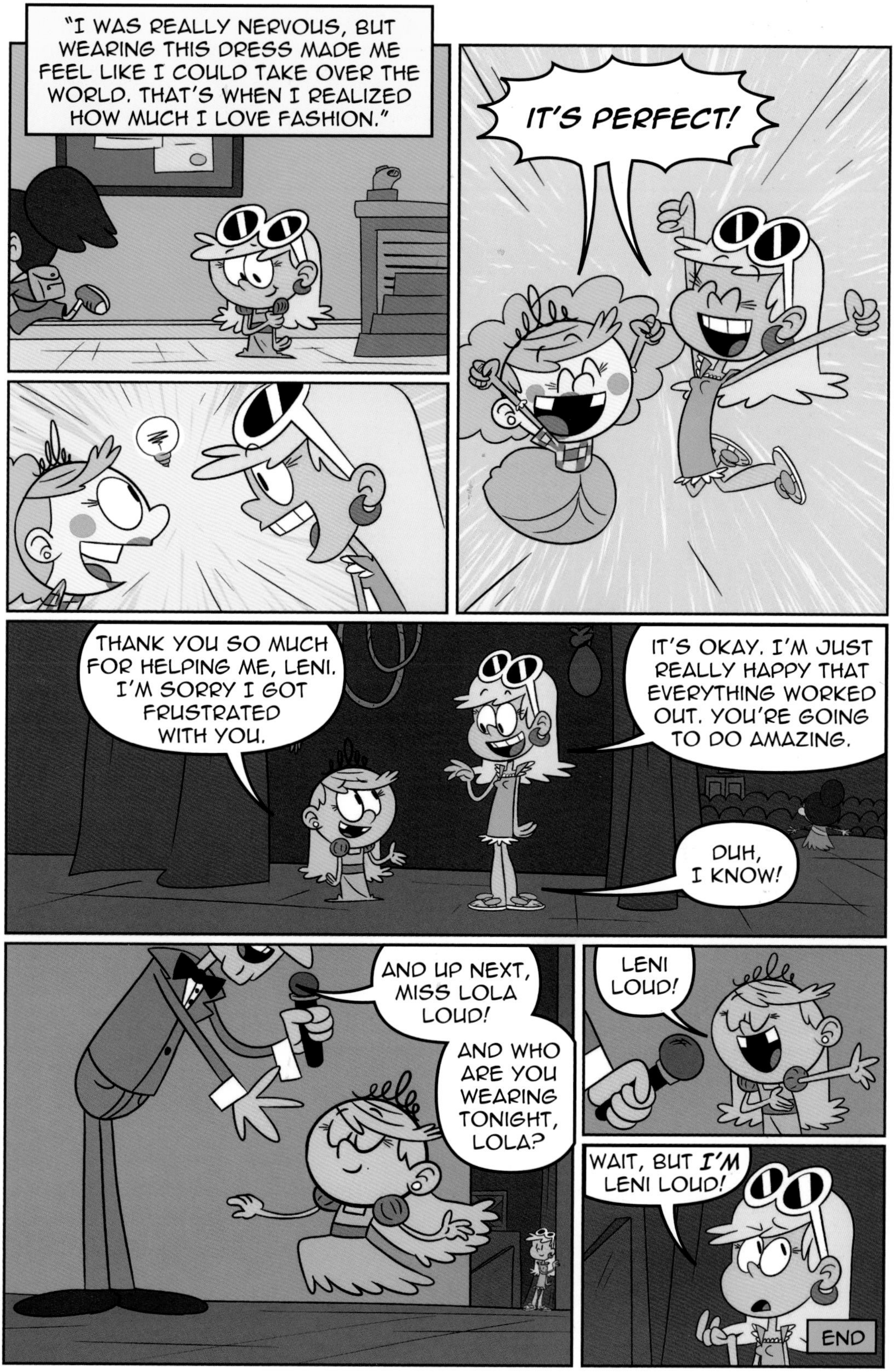
"I WAS REALLY NERVOUS, BUT WEARING THIS DRESS MADE ME FEEL LIKE I COULD TAKE OVER THE WORLD. THAT'S WHEN I REALIZED HOW MUCH I LOVE FASHION."
IT'S PERFECT!
THANK YOU SO MUCH FOR HELPING ME, LENI. I'M SORRY I GOT FRUSTRATED WITH YOU.
IT'S OKAY. I'M JUST REALLY HAPPY THAT EVERYTHING WORKED OUT. YOU'RE GOING TO DO AMAZING.
DUH, I KNOW!
AND UP NEXT, MISS LOLA LOUD!
AND WHO ARE YOU WEARING TONIGHT, LOLA?
LENI LOUD!
WAIT, BUT *I'M* LENI LOUD!
END

"FEEDING FRENZY!"

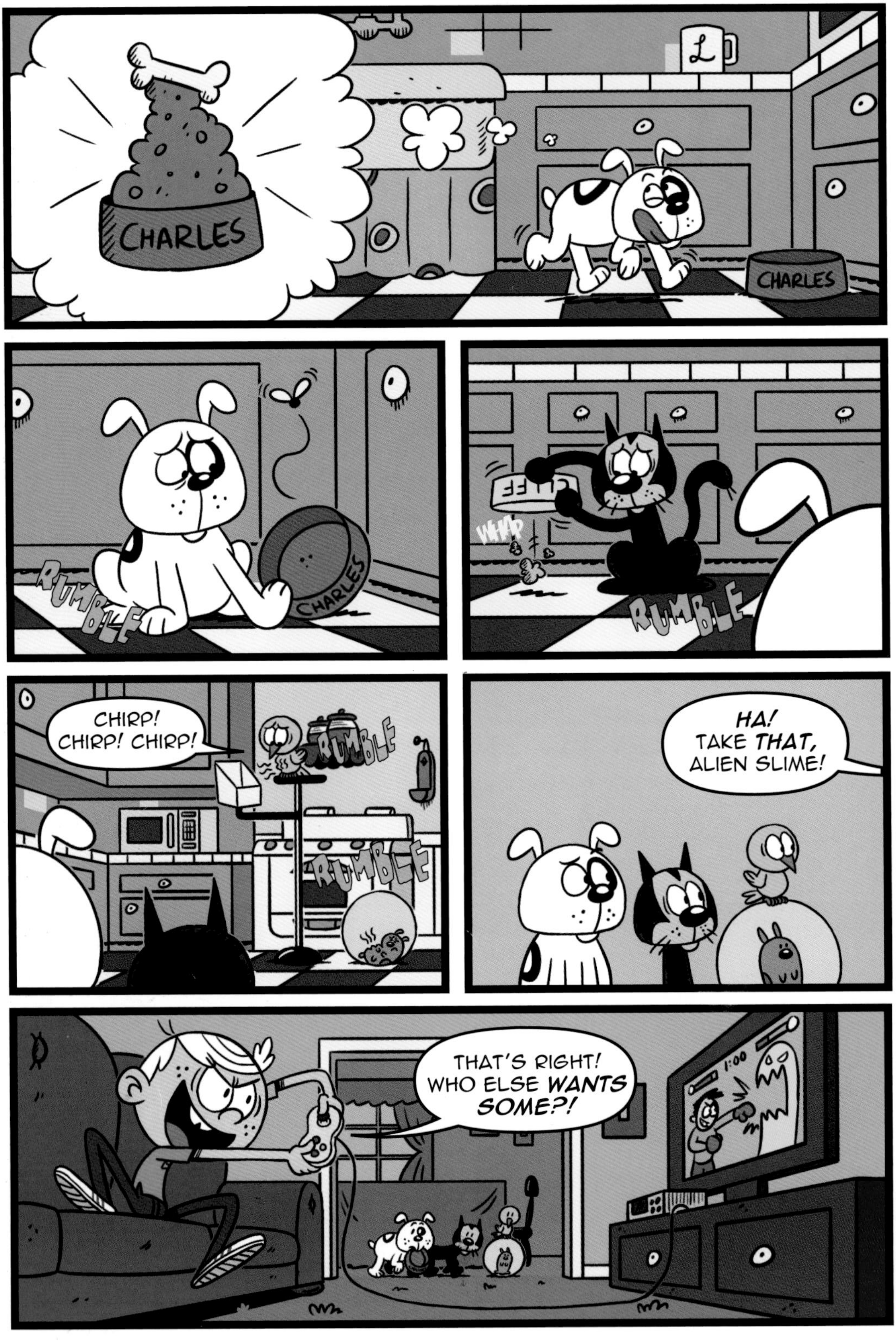
CHARLES
CHARLES
CHARLES
RUMBLE
WHAP
RUMBLE
CHIRP! CHIRP! CHIRP!
RUMBLE
RUMBLE
HA! TAKE THAT, ALIEN SLIME!
THAT'S RIGHT! WHO ELSE WANTS SOME?!
1:00

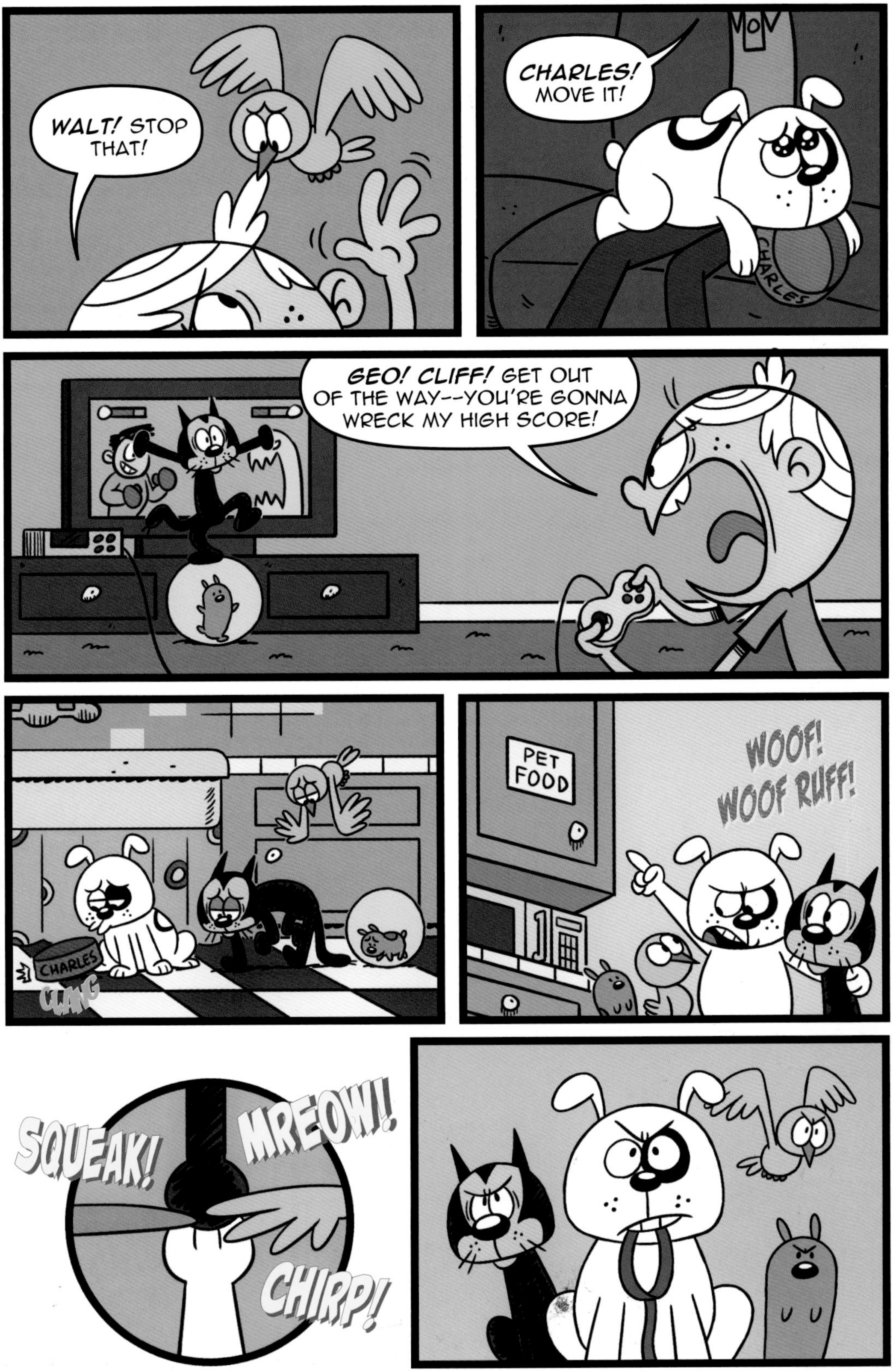
WALT! STOP THAT!
CHARLES! MOVE IT!
CHARLES
GEO! CLIFF! GET OUT OF THE WAY--YOU'RE GONNA WRECK MY HIGH SCORE!
CHARLES
CLANG
PET FOOD
WOOF! WOOF RUFF!
SQUEAK!
MREOW!!
CHIRP!

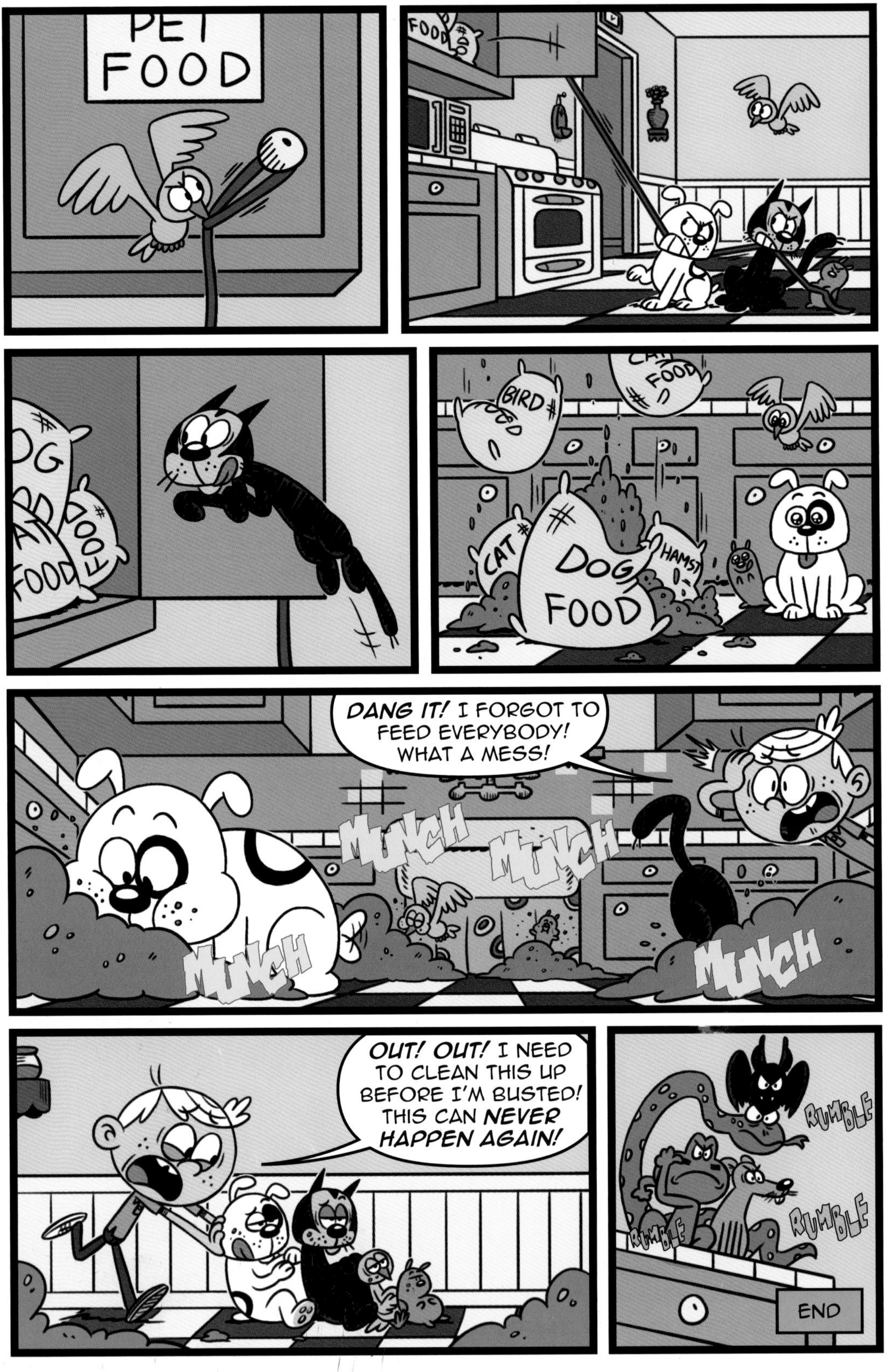
PET FOOD
FOOD
DOG FOOD
CAT FOOD
FOOD
BIRD
CAT FOOD
CAT
DOG FOOD
HAMST
DANG IT! I FORGOT TO FEED EVERYBODY! WHAT A MESS!
MUNCH
MUNCH
MUNCH
MUNCH
OUT! OUT! I NEED TO CLEAN THIS UP BEFORE I'M BUSTED! THIS CAN NEVER HAPPEN AGAIN!
RUMBLE
RUMBLE
RUMBLE
END

"SNOWBALL-ED"

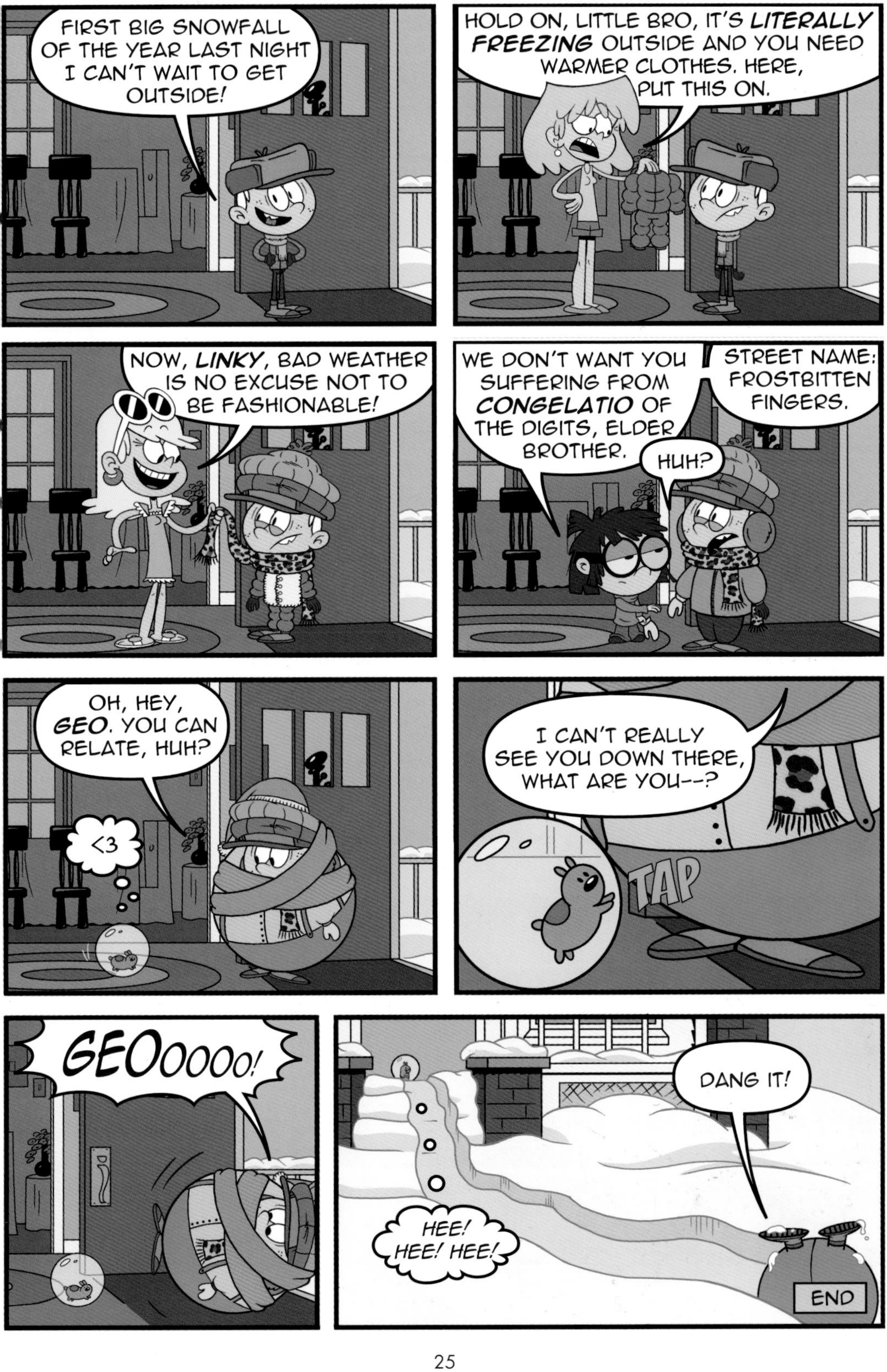
FIRST BIG SNOWFALL OF THE YEAR LAST NIGHT I CAN'T WAIT TO GET OUTSIDE!
HOLD ON, LITTLE BRO, IT'S *LITERALLY FREEZING* OUTSIDE AND YOU NEED WARMER CLOTHES. HERE, PUT THIS ON.
NOW, *LINKY*, BAD WEATHER IS NO EXCUSE NOT TO BE FASHIONABLE!
WE DON'T WANT YOU SUFFERING FROM *CONGELATIO* OF THE DIGITS, ELDER BROTHER.
STREET NAME: FROSTBITTEN FINGERS.
HUH?
OH, HEY, *GEO*. YOU CAN RELATE, HUH?
<3
I CAN'T REALLY SEE YOU DOWN THERE, WHAT ARE YOU--?
TAP
GEOoooo!
DANG IT!
HEE! HEE! HEE!
END

"SUPER HANGOUT TIME ACTIVATE!"

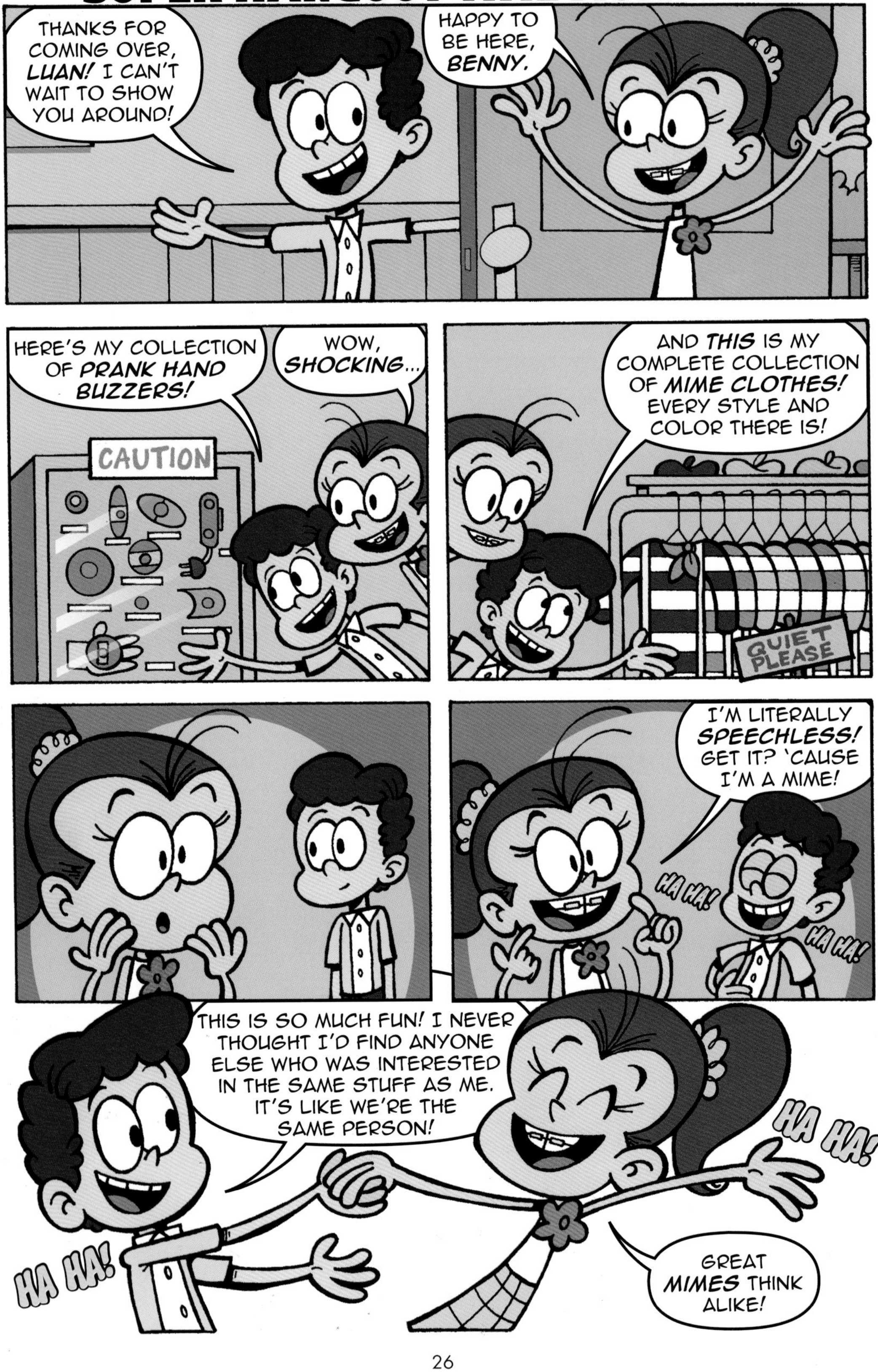
THANKS FOR COMING OVER, LUAN! I CAN'T WAIT TO SHOW YOU AROUND!
HAPPY TO BE HERE, BENNY.
HERE'S MY COLLECTION OF PRANK HAND BUZZERS!
WOW, SHOCKING...
CAUTION
AND THIS IS MY COMPLETE COLLECTION OF MIME CLOTHES! EVERY STYLE AND COLOR THERE IS!
QUIET PLEASE
I'M LITERALLY SPEECHLESS! GET IT? 'CAUSE I'M A MIME!
HA HA!
HA HA!
THIS IS SO MUCH FUN! I NEVER THOUGHT I'D FIND ANYONE ELSE WHO WAS INTERESTED IN THE SAME STUFF AS ME. IT'S LIKE WE'RE THE SAME PERSON!
HA HA!
HA HA!
GREAT MIMES THINK ALIKE!

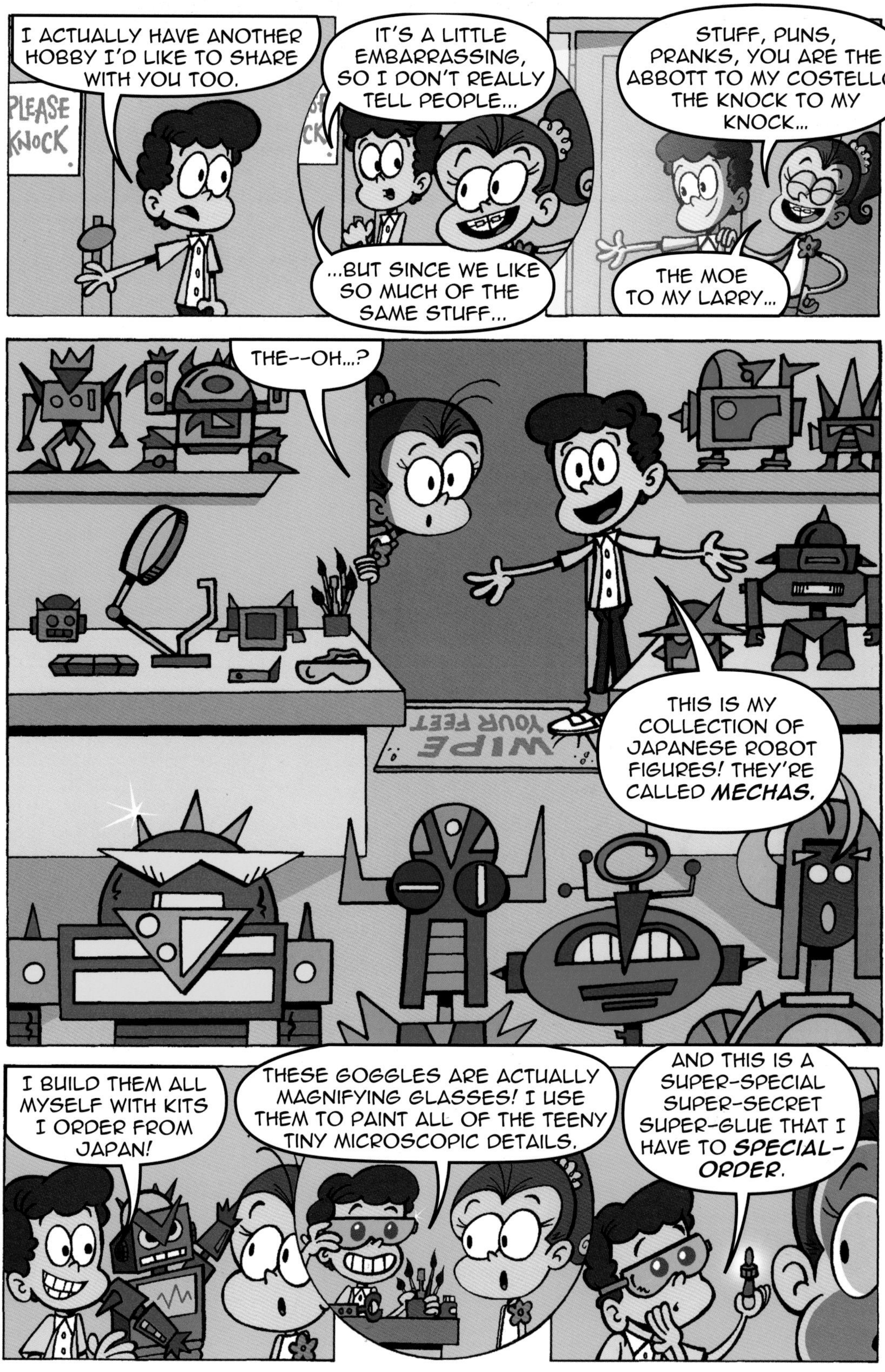
I ACTUALLY HAVE ANOTHER HOBBY I'D LIKE TO SHARE WITH YOU TOO.
PLEASE KNOCK
IT'S A LITTLE EMBARRASSING, SO I DON'T REALLY TELL PEOPLE...
...BUT SINCE WE LIKE SO MUCH OF THE SAME STUFF...
STUFF, PUNS, PRANKS, YOU ARE THE ABBOTT TO MY COSTELLO, THE KNOCK TO MY KNOCK...
THE MOE TO MY LARRY...
THE--OH...?
WIPE YOUR FEET
THIS IS MY COLLECTION OF JAPANESE ROBOT FIGURES! THEY'RE CALLED *MECHAS.*
I BUILD THEM ALL MYSELF WITH KITS I ORDER FROM JAPAN!
THESE GOGGLES ARE ACTUALLY MAGNIFYING GLASSES! I USE THEM TO PAINT ALL OF THE TEENY TINY MICROSCOPIC DETAILS.
AND THIS IS A SUPER-SPECIAL SUPER-SECRET SUPER-GLUE THAT I HAVE TO *SPECIAL-ORDER*.

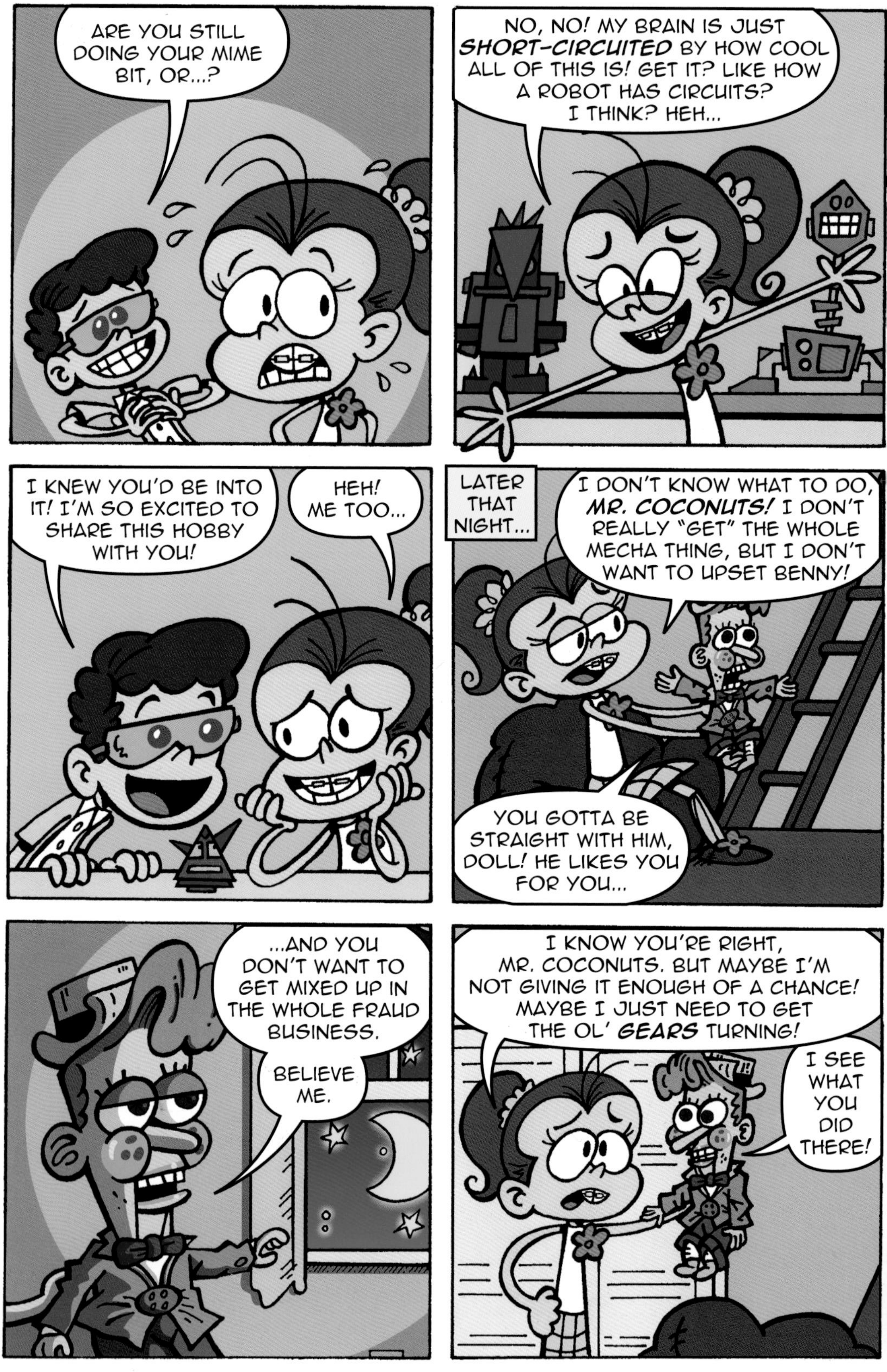
ARE YOU STILL DOING YOUR MIME BIT, OR...?
NO, NO! MY BRAIN IS JUST SHORT-CIRCUITED BY HOW COOL ALL OF THIS IS! GET IT? LIKE HOW A ROBOT HAS CIRCUITS? I THINK? HEH...
I KNEW YOU'D BE INTO IT! I'M SO EXCITED TO SHARE THIS HOBBY WITH YOU!
HEH! ME TOO...
LATER THAT NIGHT...
I DON'T KNOW WHAT TO DO, MR. COCONUTS! I DON'T REALLY "GET" THE WHOLE MECHA THING, BUT I DON'T WANT TO UPSET BENNY!
YOU GOTTA BE STRAIGHT WITH HIM, DOLL! HE LIKES YOU FOR YOU...
...AND YOU DON'T WANT TO GET MIXED UP IN THE WHOLE FRAUD BUSINESS.
BELIEVE ME.
I KNOW YOU'RE RIGHT, MR. COCONUTS. BUT MAYBE I'M NOT GIVING IT ENOUGH OF A CHANCE! MAYBE I JUST NEED TO GET THE OL' GEARS TURNING!
I SEE WHAT YOU DID THERE!

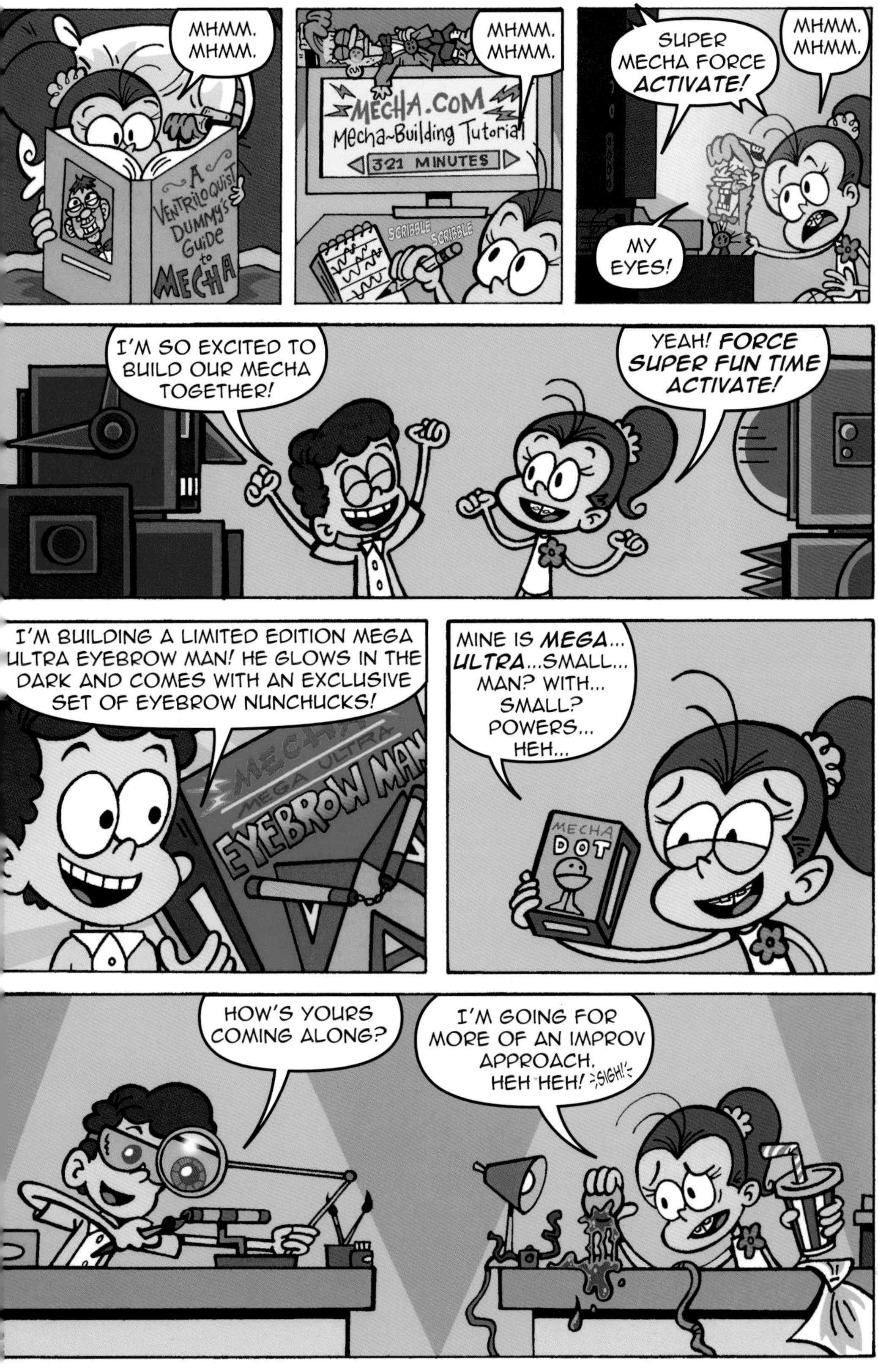
MHMM. MHMM.
A VENTRILOQUIST DUMMY'S GUIDE to MECHA
MECHA.COM
Mecha-Building Tutorial
321 MINUTES
MHMM. MHMM.
SCRIBBLE
SCRIBBLE
SUPER MECHA FORCE ACTIVATE!
MHMM. MHMM.
MY EYES!
I'M SO EXCITED TO BUILD OUR MECHA TOGETHER!
YEAH! FORCE SUPER FUN TIME ACTIVATE!
I'M BUILDING A LIMITED EDITION MEGA ULTRA EYEBROW MAN! HE GLOWS IN THE DARK AND COMES WITH AN EXCLUSIVE SET OF EYEBROW NUNCHUCKS!
MEGA ULTRA EYEBROW MAN
MINE IS MEGA... ULTRA...SMALL... MAN? WITH... SMALL? POWERS... HEH...
MECHA DOT
HOW'S YOURS COMING ALONG?
I'M GOING FOR MORE OF AN IMPROV APPROACH. HEH HEH! SIGH!

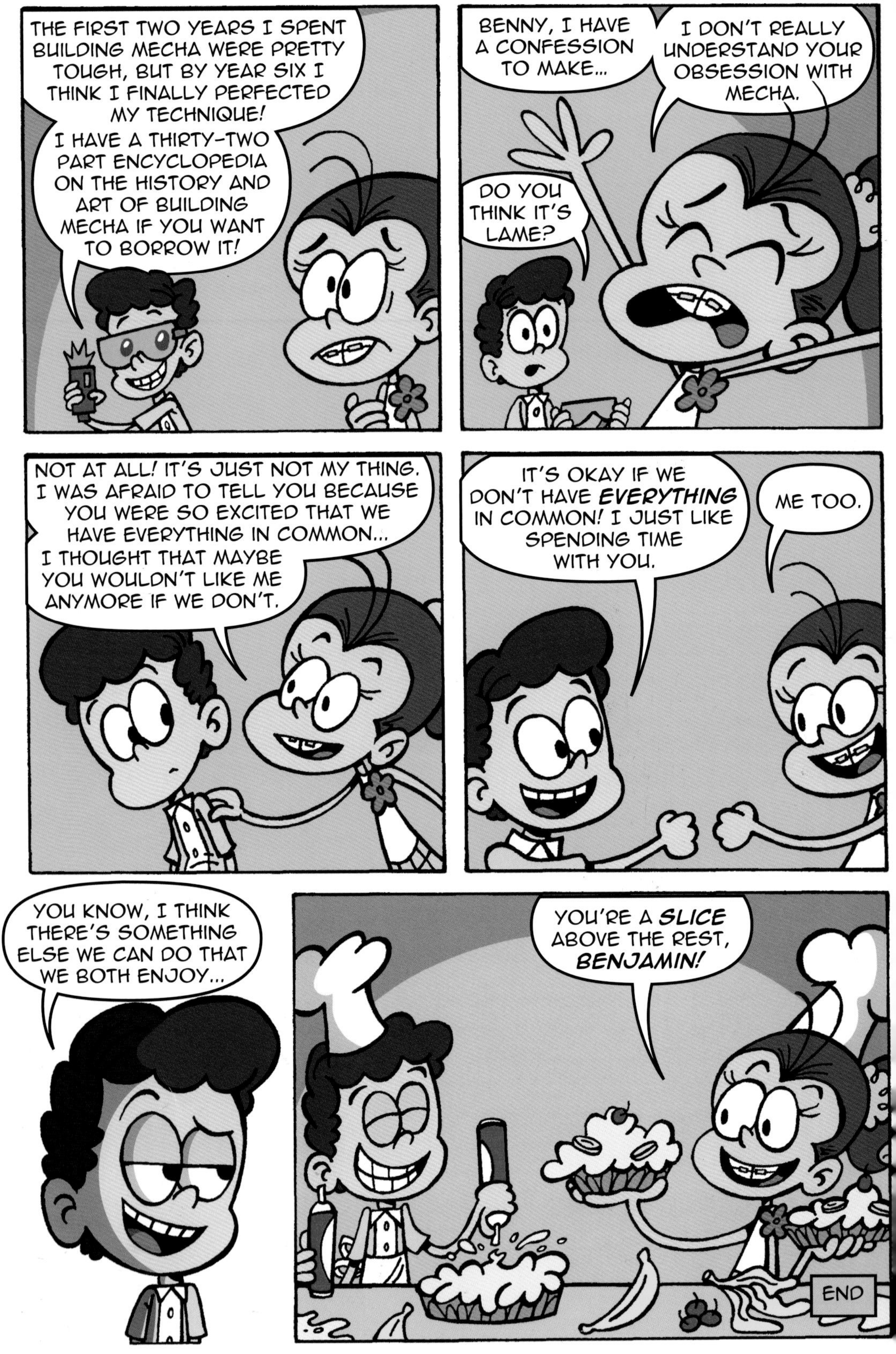
THE FIRST TWO YEARS I SPENT BUILDING MECHA WERE PRETTY TOUGH, BUT BY YEAR SIX I THINK I FINALLY PERFECTED MY TECHNIQUE!
I HAVE A THIRTY-TWO PART ENCYCLOPEDIA ON THE HISTORY AND ART OF BUILDING MECHA IF YOU WANT TO BORROW IT!
BENNY, I HAVE A CONFESSION TO MAKE...
I DON'T REALLY UNDERSTAND YOUR OBSESSION WITH MECHA.
DO YOU THINK IT'S LAME?
NOT AT ALL! IT'S JUST NOT MY THING. I WAS AFRAID TO TELL YOU BECAUSE YOU WERE SO EXCITED THAT WE HAVE EVERYTHING IN COMMON...
I THOUGHT THAT MAYBE YOU WOULDN'T LIKE ME ANYMORE IF WE DON'T.
IT'S OKAY IF WE DON'T HAVE **EVERYTHING** IN COMMON! I JUST LIKE SPENDING TIME WITH YOU.
ME TOO.
YOU KNOW, I THINK THERE'S SOMETHING ELSE WE CAN DO THAT WE BOTH ENJOY...
YOU'RE A ***SLICE*** ABOVE THE REST, ***BENJAMIN!***
END

"STUDY BUDDIES"

GET YOUR HEAD IN THE GAME, *LYNN.* THIS IS NO TIME TO CHOKE! YOU CAN DO THIS!

YOU'RE A CHAMPION. C-H-A-M-P-E-O-N-N.

LET'S SEE...C...

≶ARGH!≷ WRONG AGAIN.

GET IT TOGETHER, LYNN-ER! LOSING IS FOR *LOSERS!*

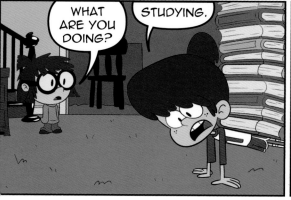

WHAT ARE YOU DOING?

STUDYING.

...

I WON'T QUESTION IT.

I HAVE A SPELLING BEE TOMORROW AND I'M GOING TO TRIUMPH IF IT'S THE LAST THING I DO! T-R-Y-U-M-F.
THAT'S NOT HOW YOU SPELL--
I KNOW!
I MEAN, WHO CARES ABOUT SPELLING ANYWAY?
IF I COULD CHALLENGE SPELLING TO A ONE-ON-ONE B-BALL GAME, I'D TOTALLY WIN.
BUT IT'S NOT A BASKETBALL GAME. IT'S A SPELLING BEE. AND STATISTICALLY SPEAKING, IF YOU CAN'T SPELL THEN YOU'RE PROBABLY GOING TO LOSE.
L-O-O-S-E?
YEAH, YOU'RE GOING TO DO HORRIBLY.
WHO ASKED YOU ANYWAY?
HEY, WHO WANTS TO RACE? GET READY TO EAT MY DUST!

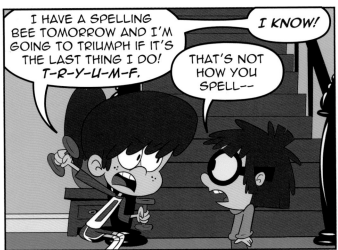

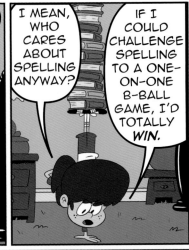

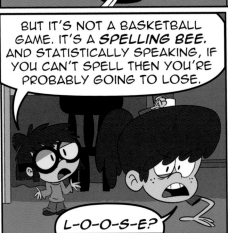

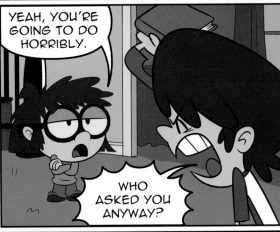

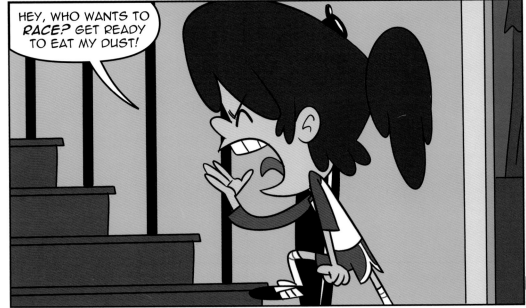

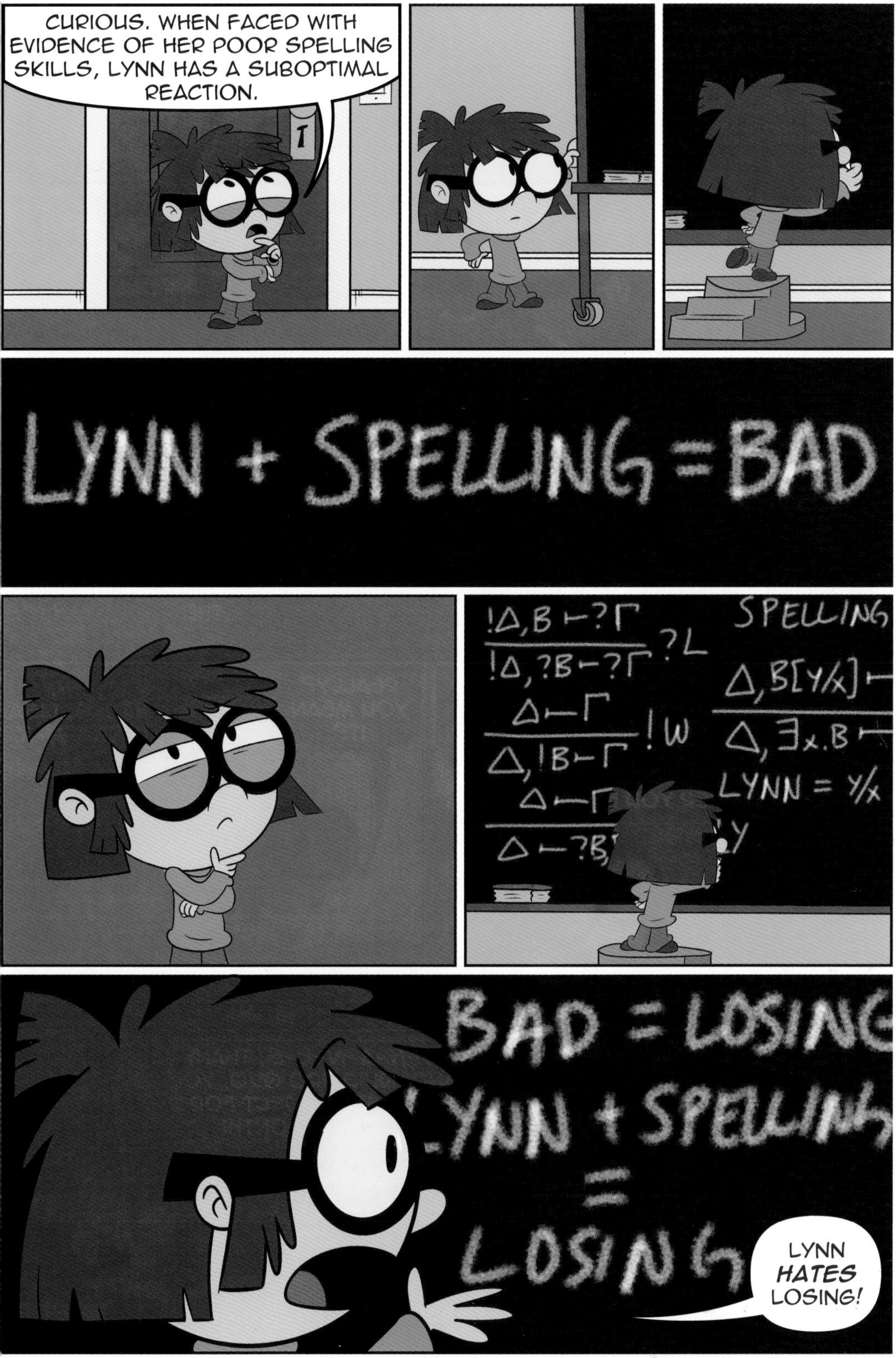

CURIOUS. WHEN FACED WITH EVIDENCE OF HER POOR SPELLING SKILLS, LYNN HAS A SUBOPTIMAL REACTION.
LYNN + SPELLING = BAD
SPELLING
LYNN = Y/X
BAD = LOSING
LYNN + SPELLING = LOSING
LYNN HATES LOSING!

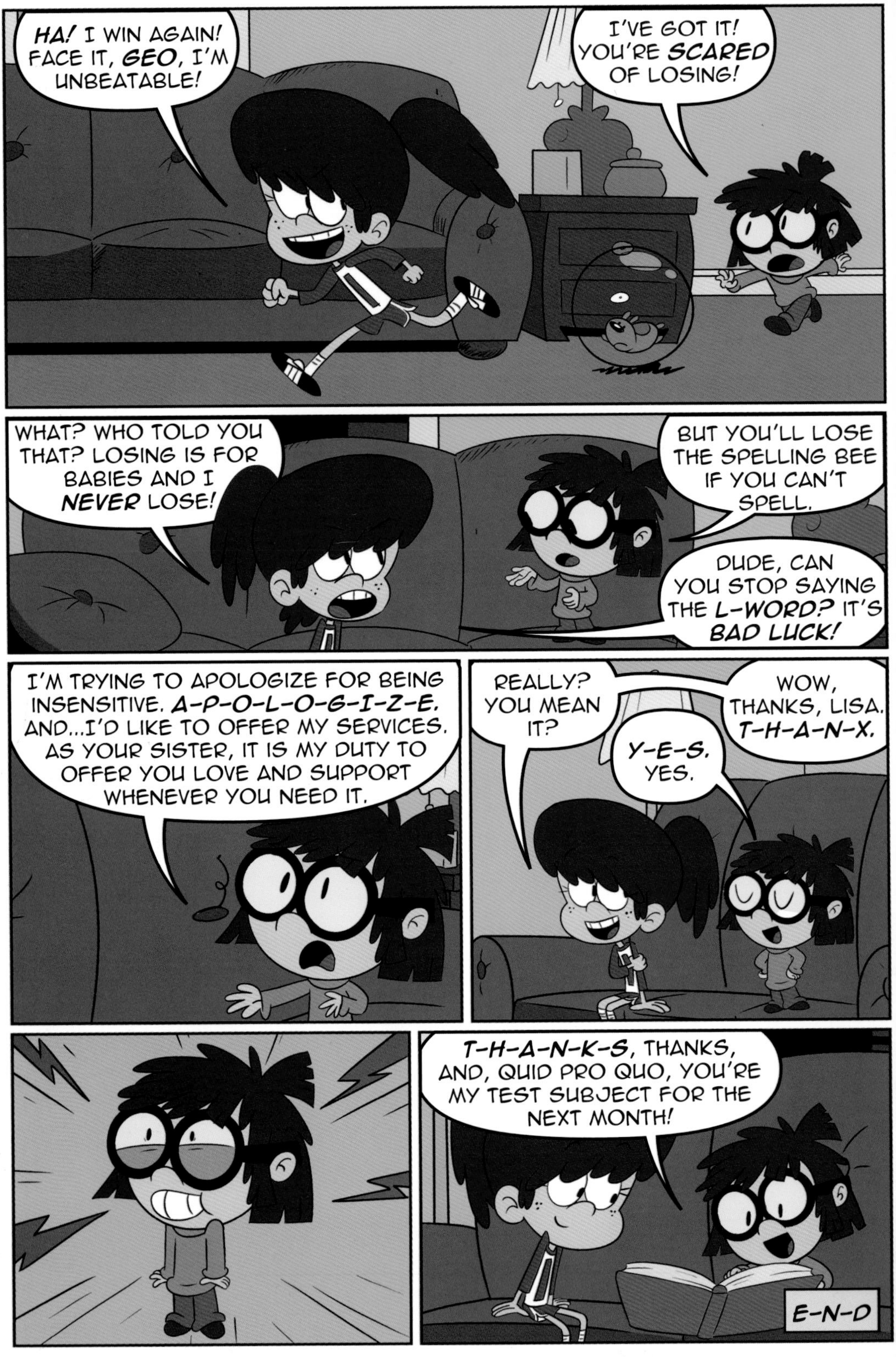
HA! I WIN AGAIN! FACE IT, GEO, I'M UNBEATABLE!
I'VE GOT IT! YOU'RE SCARED OF LOSING!
WHAT? WHO TOLD YOU THAT? LOSING IS FOR BABIES AND I NEVER LOSE!
BUT YOU'LL LOSE THE SPELLING BEE IF YOU CAN'T SPELL.
DUDE, CAN YOU STOP SAYING THE L-WORD? IT'S BAD LUCK!
I'M TRYING TO APOLOGIZE FOR BEING INSENSITIVE. A-P-O-L-O-G-I-Z-E. AND...I'D LIKE TO OFFER MY SERVICES. AS YOUR SISTER, IT IS MY DUTY TO OFFER YOU LOVE AND SUPPORT WHENEVER YOU NEED IT.
REALLY? YOU MEAN IT?
Y-E-S. YES.
WOW, THANKS, LISA. T-H-A-N-X.
T-H-A-N-K-S, THANKS, AND, QUID PRO QUO, YOU'RE MY TEST SUBJECT FOR THE NEXT MONTH!
E-N-D

CATCHING UP WITH THE CASAGRANDES!

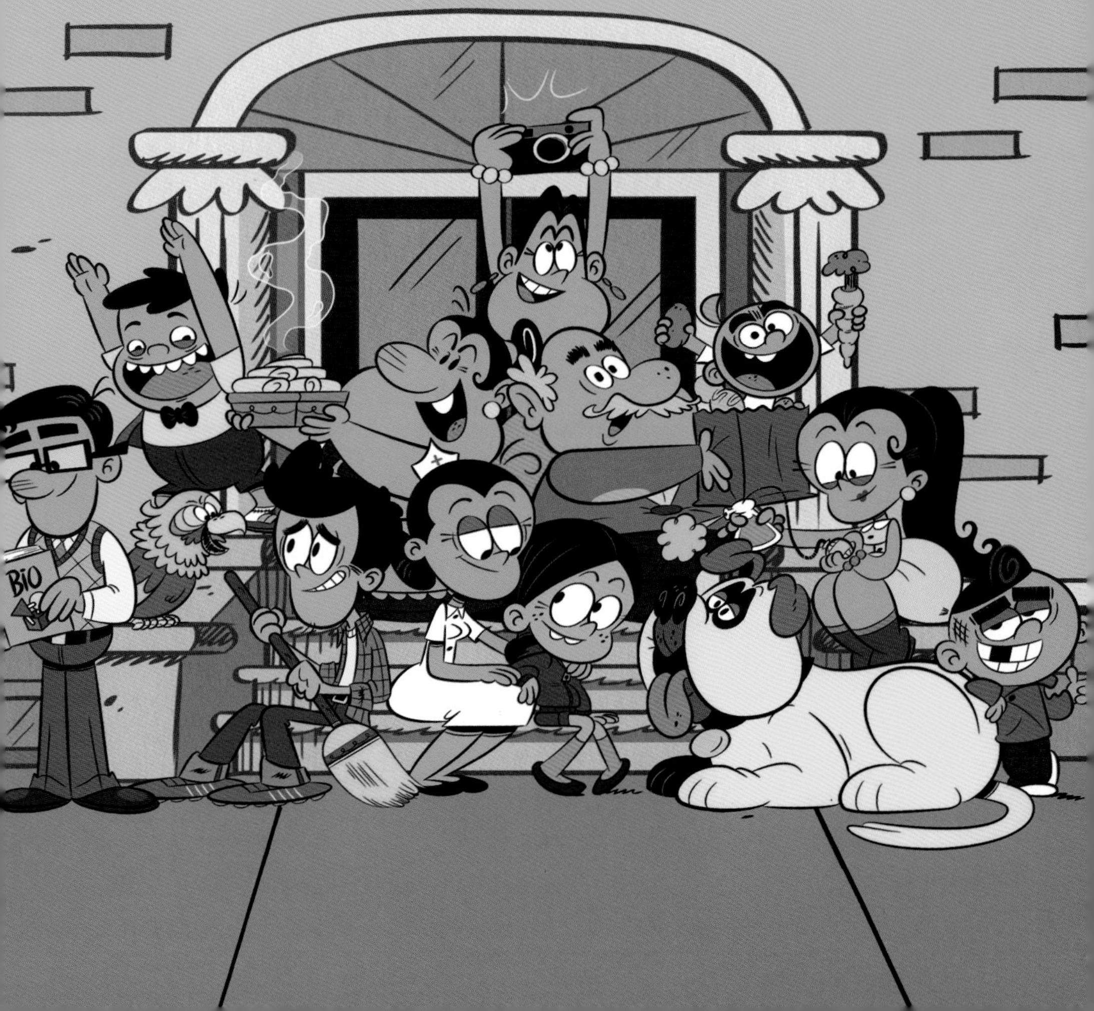
BIO

"RAIN, RAIN, HERE TO STAY"

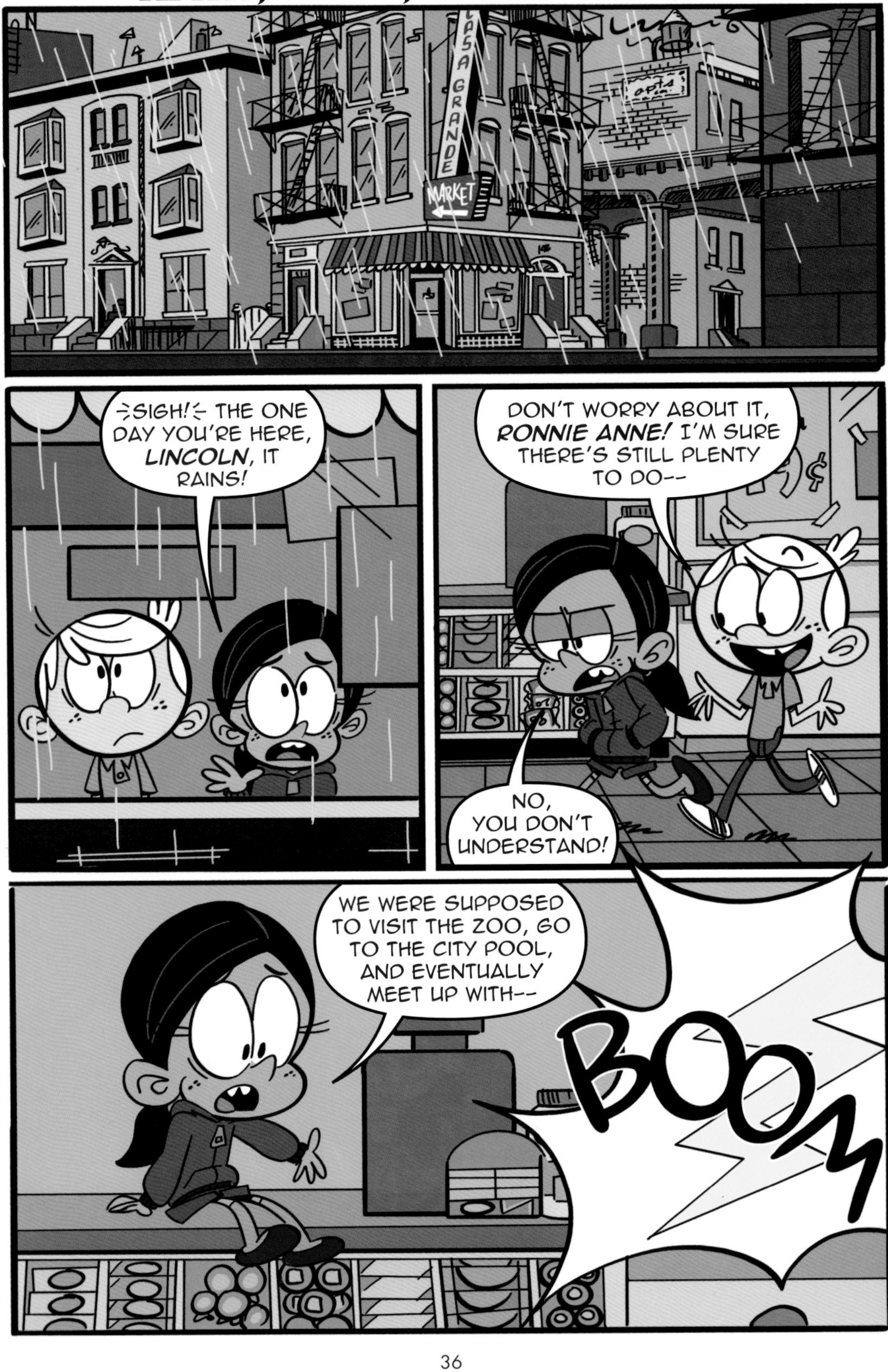
CASA GRANDE
MARKET
≑SIGH!≑ THE ONE DAY YOU'RE HERE, LINCOLN, IT RAINS!
DON'T WORRY ABOUT IT, RONNIE ANNE! I'M SURE THERE'S STILL PLENTY TO DO--
NO, YOU DON'T UNDERSTAND!
WE WERE SUPPOSED TO VISIT THE ZOO, GO TO THE CITY POOL, AND EVENTUALLY MEET UP WITH--
BOOM

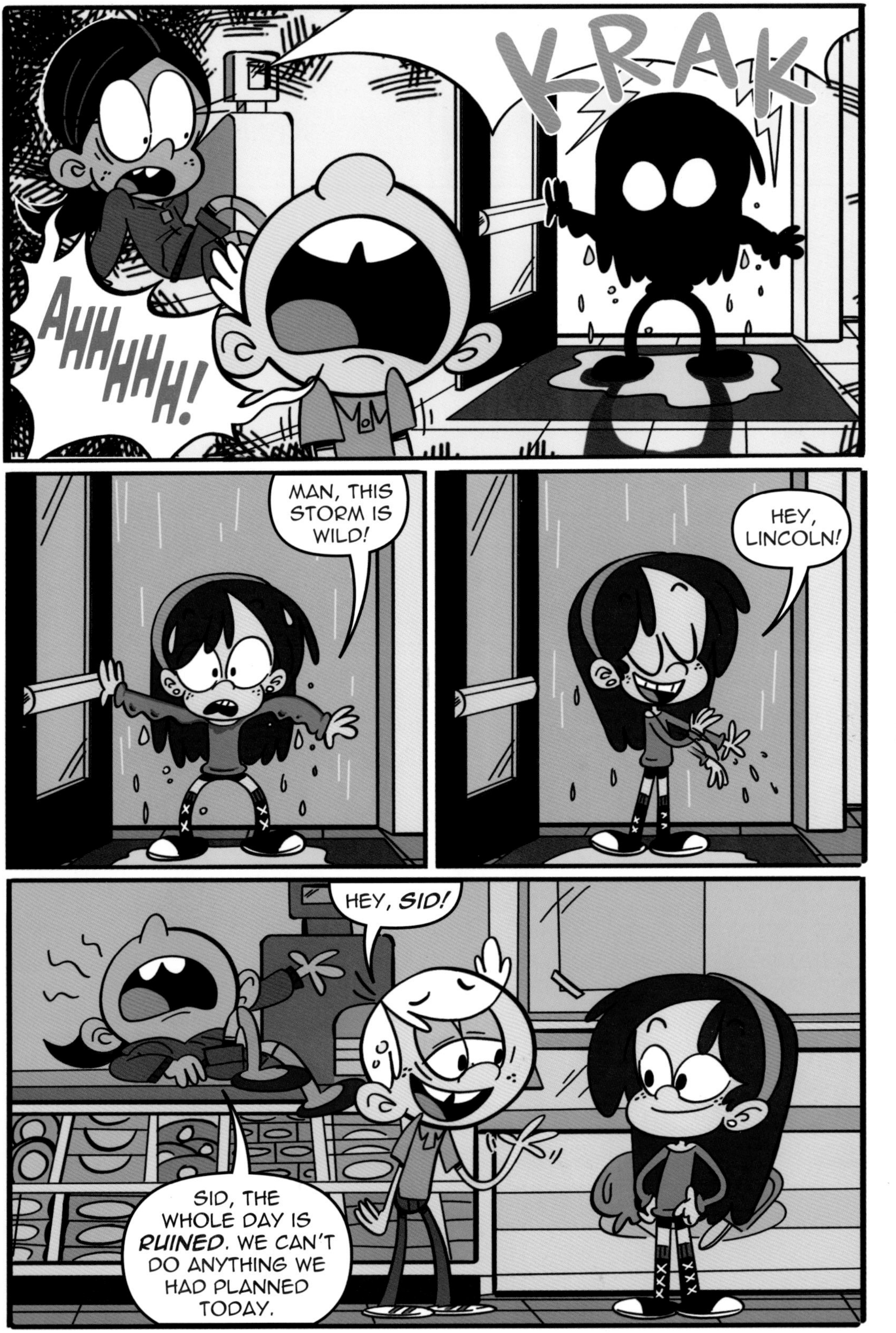
KRAK
AHHHHHH!
MAN, THIS STORM IS WILD!
HEY, LINCOLN!
HEY, SID!
SID, THE WHOLE DAY IS RUINED. WE CAN'T DO ANYTHING WE HAD PLANNED TODAY.

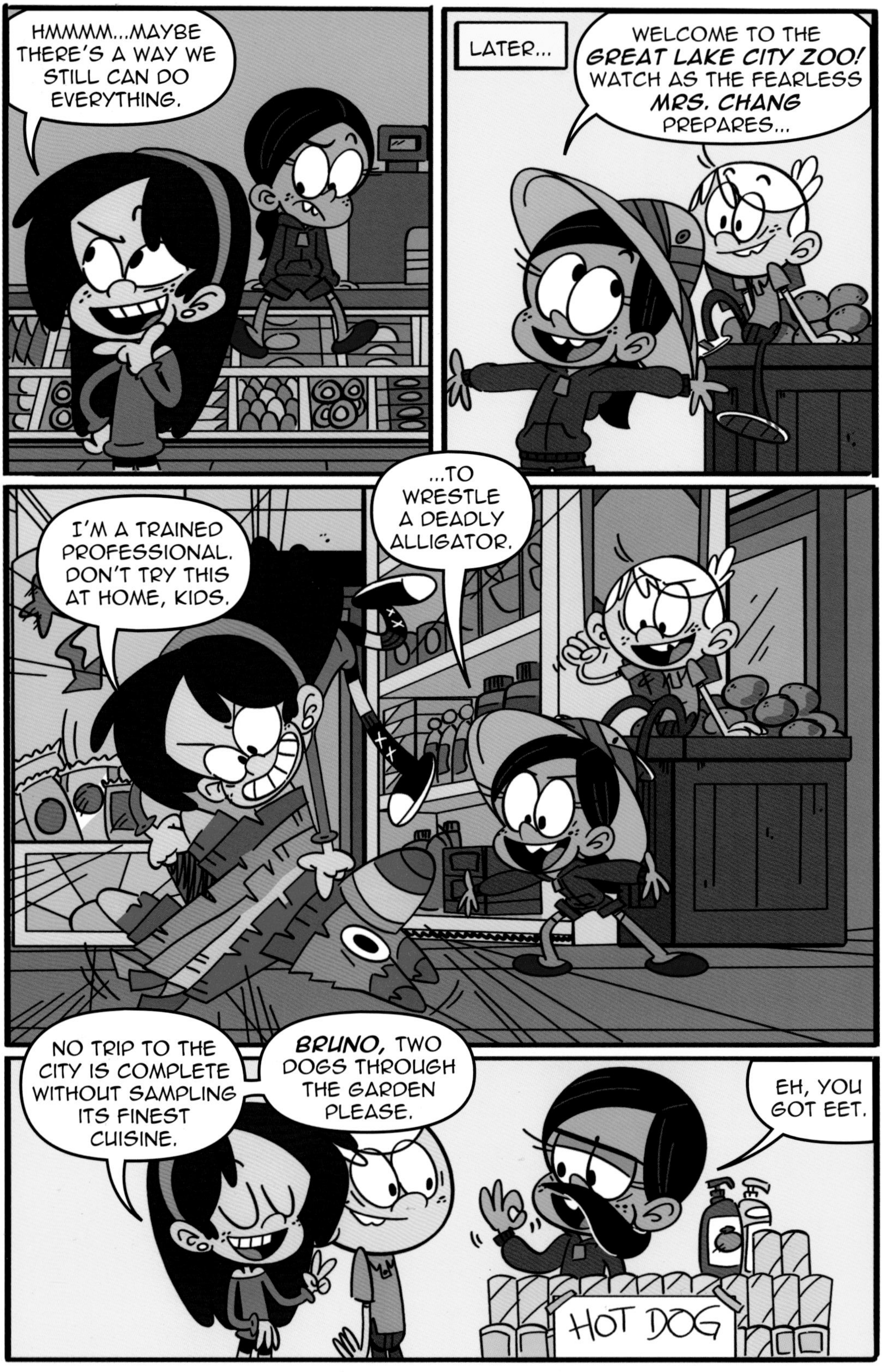
HMMMM...MAYBE THERE'S A WAY WE STILL CAN DO EVERYTHING.
LATER...
WELCOME TO THE ***GREAT LAKE CITY ZOO!*** WATCH AS THE FEARLESS ***MRS. CHANG*** PREPARES...
I'M A TRAINED PROFESSIONAL. DON'T TRY THIS AT HOME, KIDS.
...TO WRESTLE A DEADLY ALLIGATOR.
NO TRIP TO THE CITY IS COMPLETE WITHOUT SAMPLING ITS FINEST CUISINE.
BRUNO, TWO DOGS THROUGH THE GARDEN PLEASE.
EH, YOU GOT EET.
HOT DOG

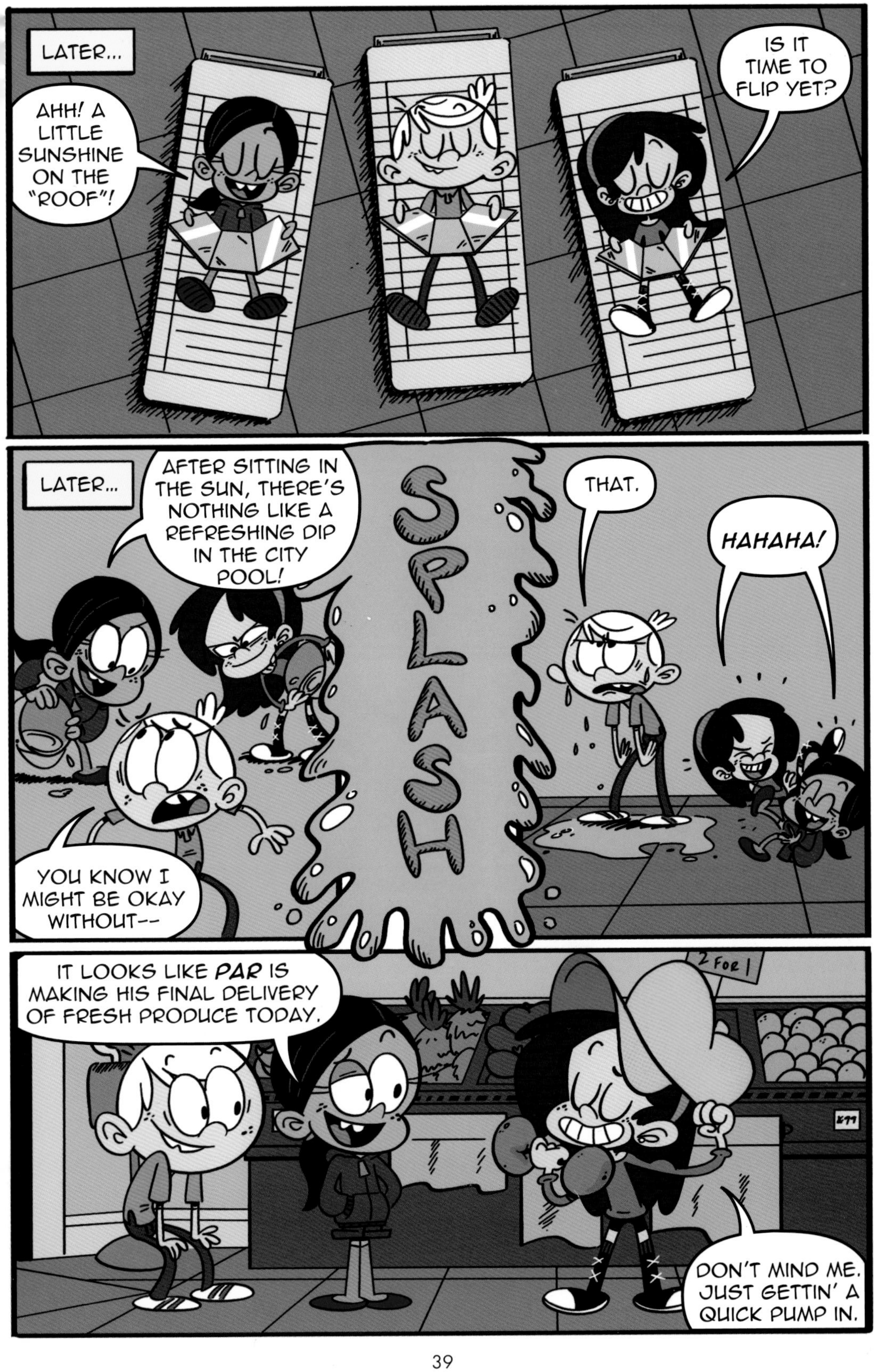
LATER...
AHH! A LITTLE SUNSHINE ON THE "ROOF"!
IS IT TIME TO FLIP YET?
LATER...
AFTER SITTING IN THE SUN, THERE'S NOTHING LIKE A REFRESHING DIP IN THE CITY POOL!
YOU KNOW I MIGHT BE OKAY WITHOUT--
SPLASH
THAT.
HAHAHA!
IT LOOKS LIKE PAR IS MAKING HIS FINAL DELIVERY OF FRESH PRODUCE TODAY.
2 FOR 1
DON'T MIND ME. JUST GETTIN' A QUICK PUMP IN.

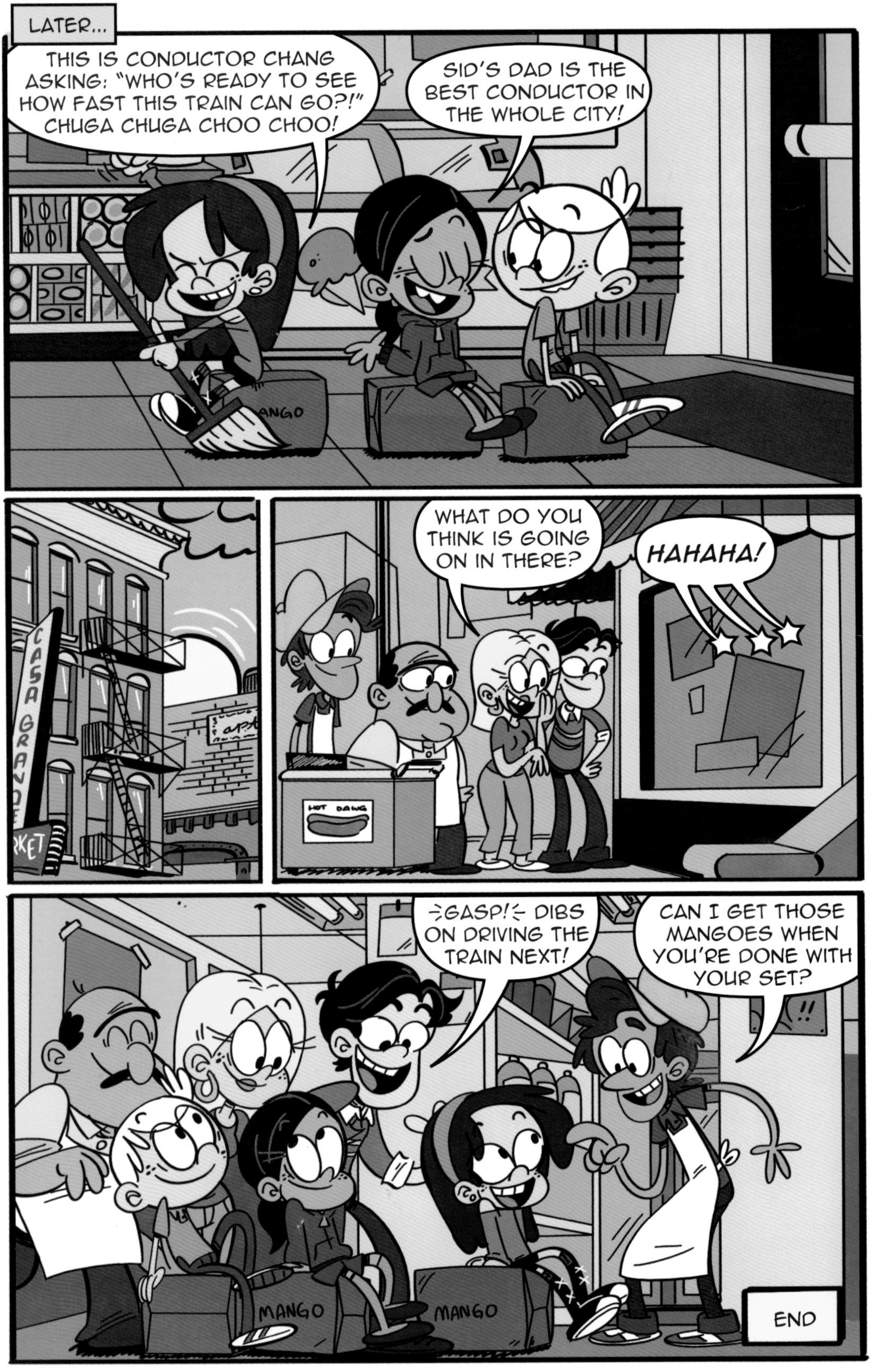
LATER...
THIS IS CONDUCTOR CHANG ASKING: "WHO'S READY TO SEE HOW FAST THIS TRAIN CAN GO?!" CHUGA CHUGA CHOO CHOO!
SID'S DAD IS THE BEST CONDUCTOR IN THE WHOLE CITY!
MANGO
CASA GRANDE
RKET
WHAT DO YOU THINK IS GOING ON IN THERE?
HAHAHA!
HOT DAWG
GASP! DIBS ON DRIVING THE TRAIN NEXT!
CAN I GET THOSE MANGOES WHEN YOU'RE DONE WITH YOUR SET?
MANGO
MANGO
END

"CITY TRICKERS"

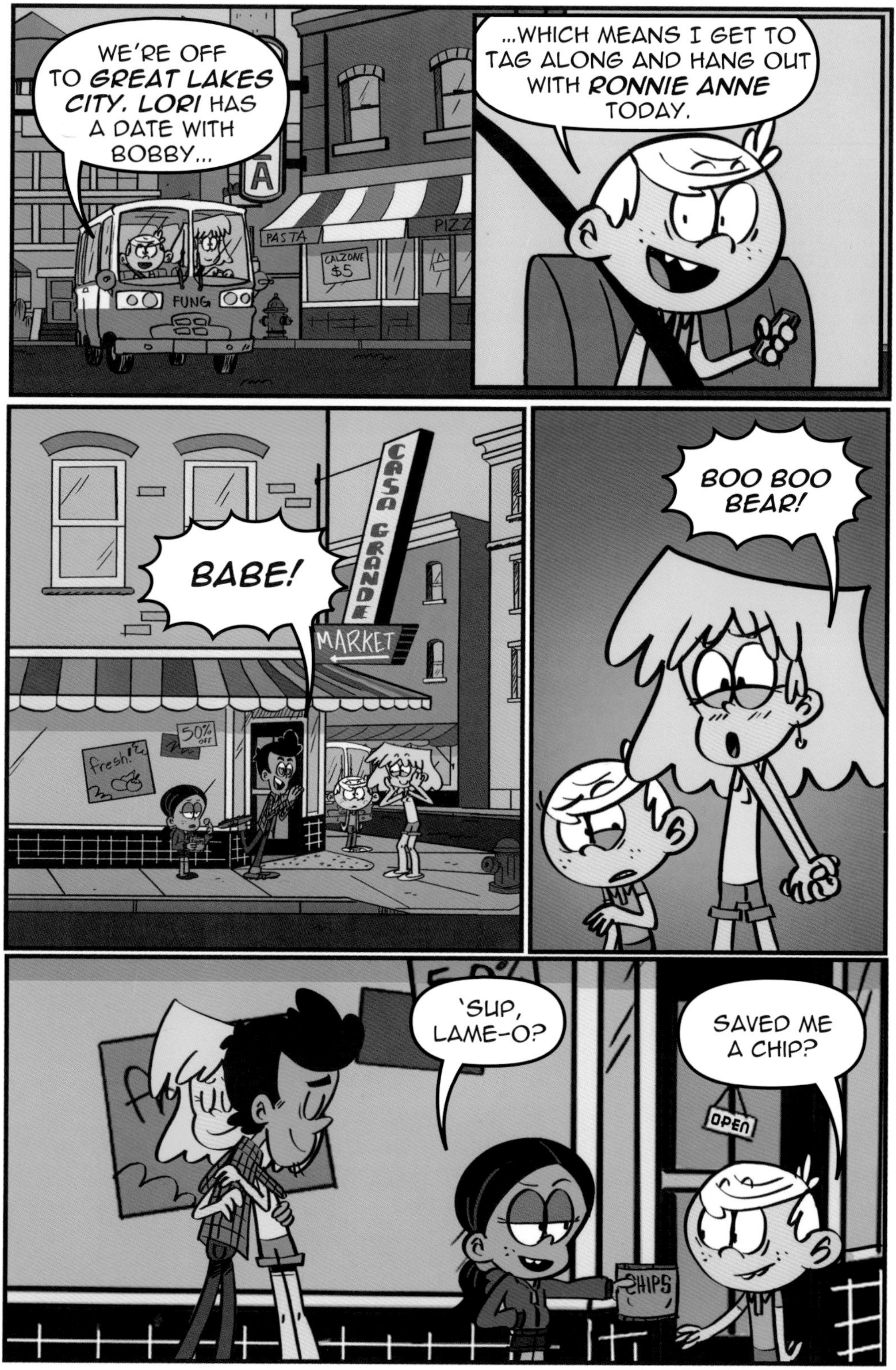

WE'RE OFF TO GREAT LAKES CITY. LORI HAS A DATE WITH BOBBY...
A
PASTA
PIZZ
CALZONE $5
FUNG
...WHICH MEANS I GET TO TAG ALONG AND HANG OUT WITH RONNIE ANNE TODAY.
CASA GRANDE
MARKET
BABE!
50% OFF
fresh!
BOO BOO BEAR!
'SUP, LAME-O?
SAVED ME A CHIP?
OPEN
CHIPS

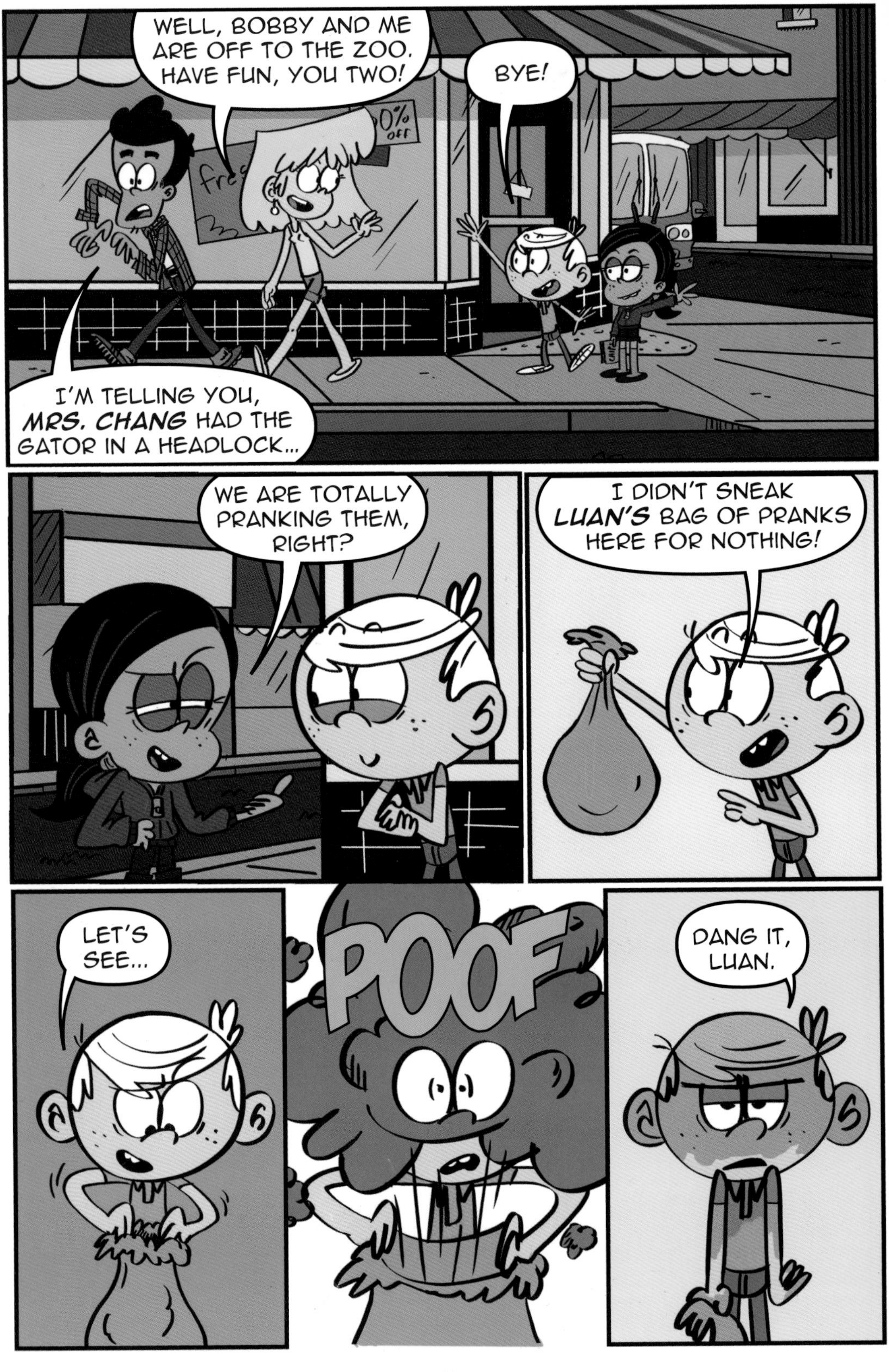
WELL, BOBBY AND ME ARE OFF TO THE ZOO. HAVE FUN, YOU TWO!
BYE!
I'M TELLING YOU, MRS. CHANG HAD THE GATOR IN A HEADLOCK...
WE ARE TOTALLY PRANKING THEM, RIGHT?
I DIDN'T SNEAK LUAN'S BAG OF PRANKS HERE FOR NOTHING!
LET'S SEE...
POOF
DANG IT, LUAN.

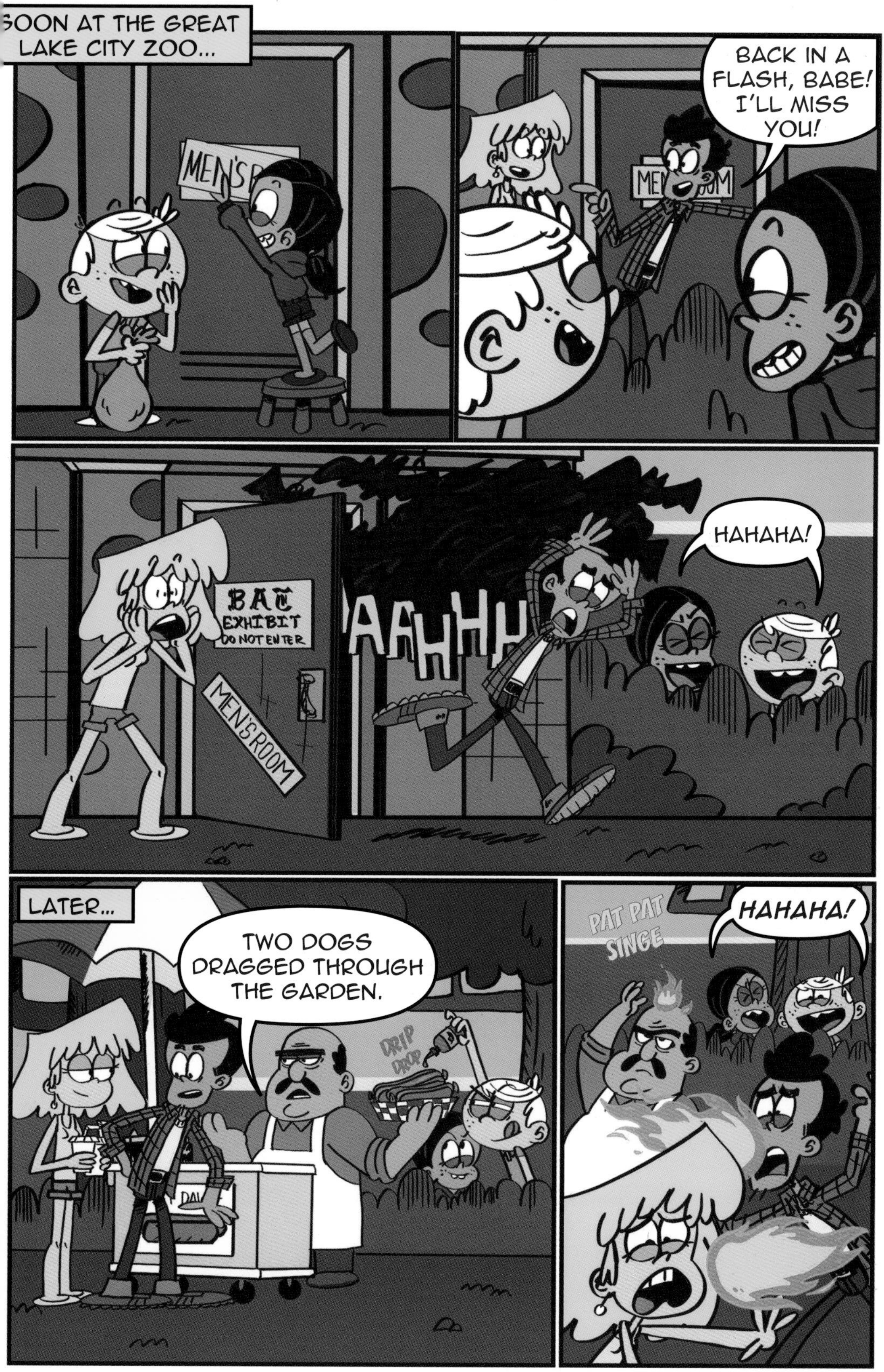
SOON AT THE GREAT LAKE CITY ZOO...
BACK IN A FLASH, BABE! I'LL MISS YOU!
BAT EXHIBIT DO NOT ENTER
MEN'S ROOM
AAHHH
HAHAHA!
LATER...
TWO DOGS DRAGGED THROUGH THE GARDEN.
DRIP DROP
PAT PAT SINGE
HAHAHA!

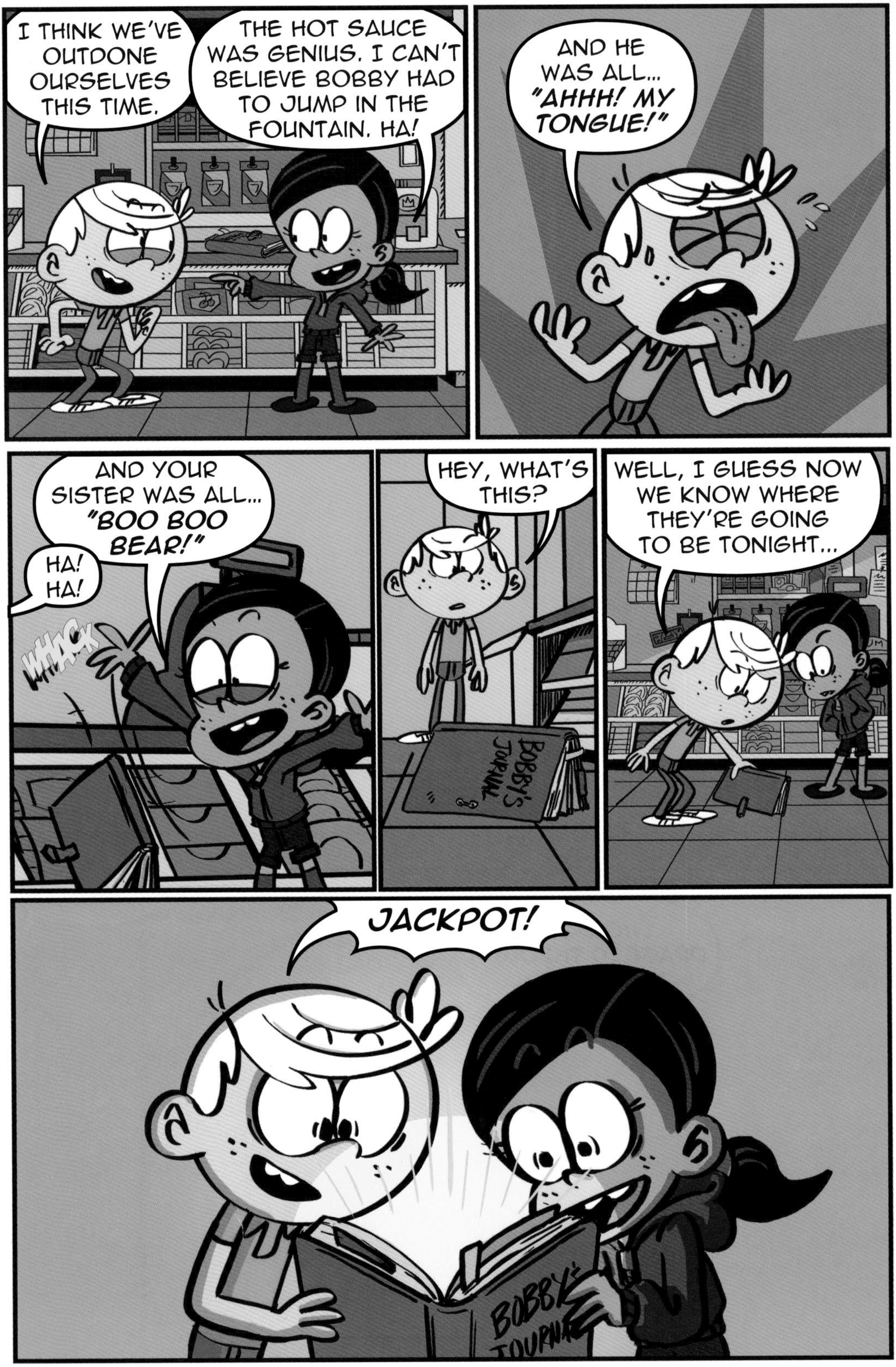
I THINK WE'VE OUTDONE OURSELVES THIS TIME.
THE HOT SAUCE WAS GENIUS. I CAN'T BELIEVE BOBBY HAD TO JUMP IN THE FOUNTAIN. HA!
AND HE WAS ALL... "AHHH! MY TONGUE!"
AND YOUR SISTER WAS ALL... "BOO BOO BEAR!"
HA! HA!
WHACK
HEY, WHAT'S THIS?
BOBBY'S JOURNAL
WELL, I GUESS NOW WE KNOW WHERE THEY'RE GOING TO BE TONIGHT...
JACKPOT!
BOBBY'S JOURNAL

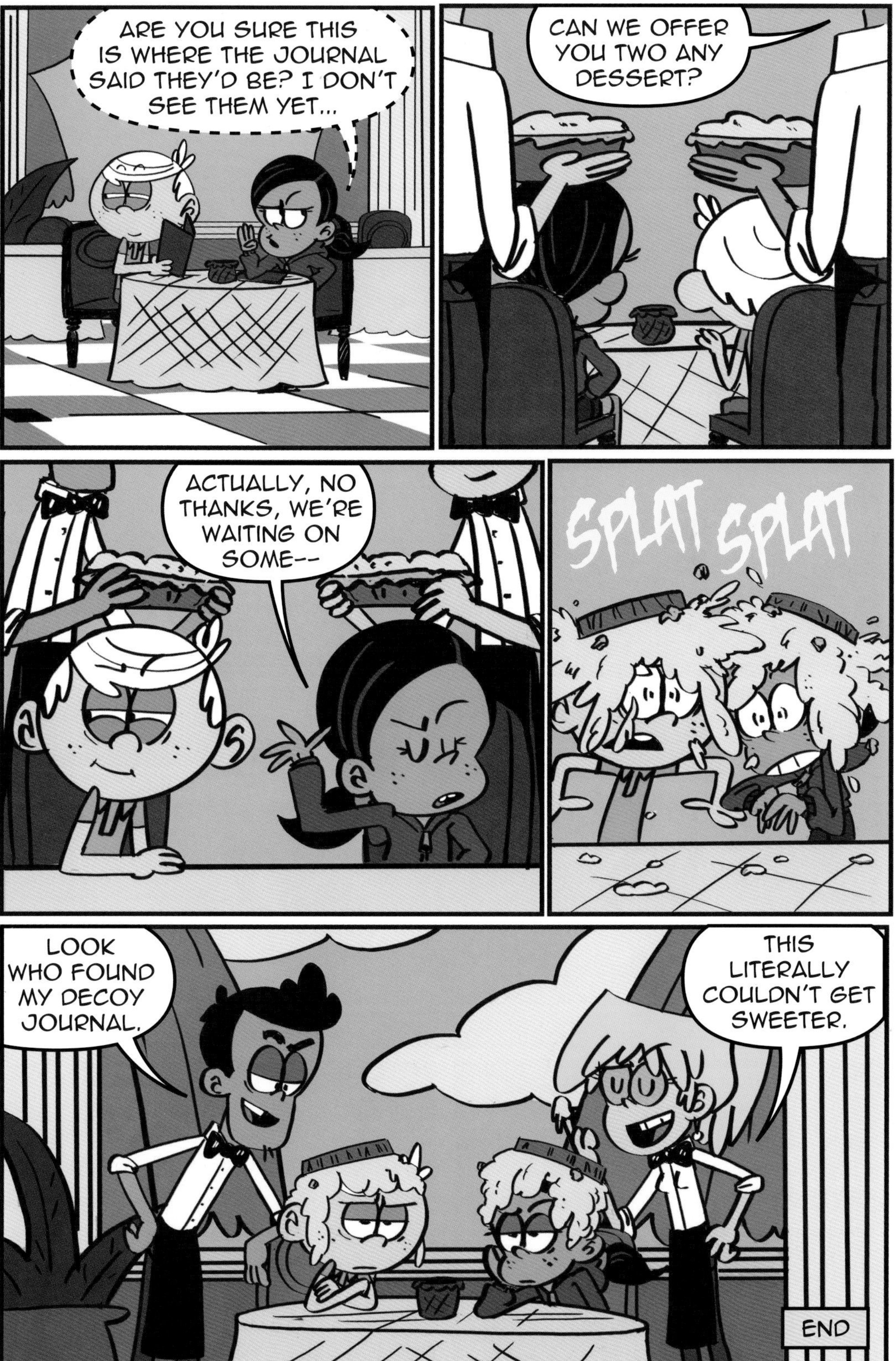
ARE YOU SURE THIS IS WHERE THE JOURNAL SAID THEY'D BE? I DON'T SEE THEM YET...
CAN WE OFFER YOU TWO ANY DESSERT?
ACTUALLY, NO THANKS, WE'RE WAITING ON SOME--
SPLAT SPLAT
LOOK WHO FOUND MY DECOY JOURNAL.
THIS LITERALLY COULDN'T GET SWEETER.
END

"PARTY ANIMALS"

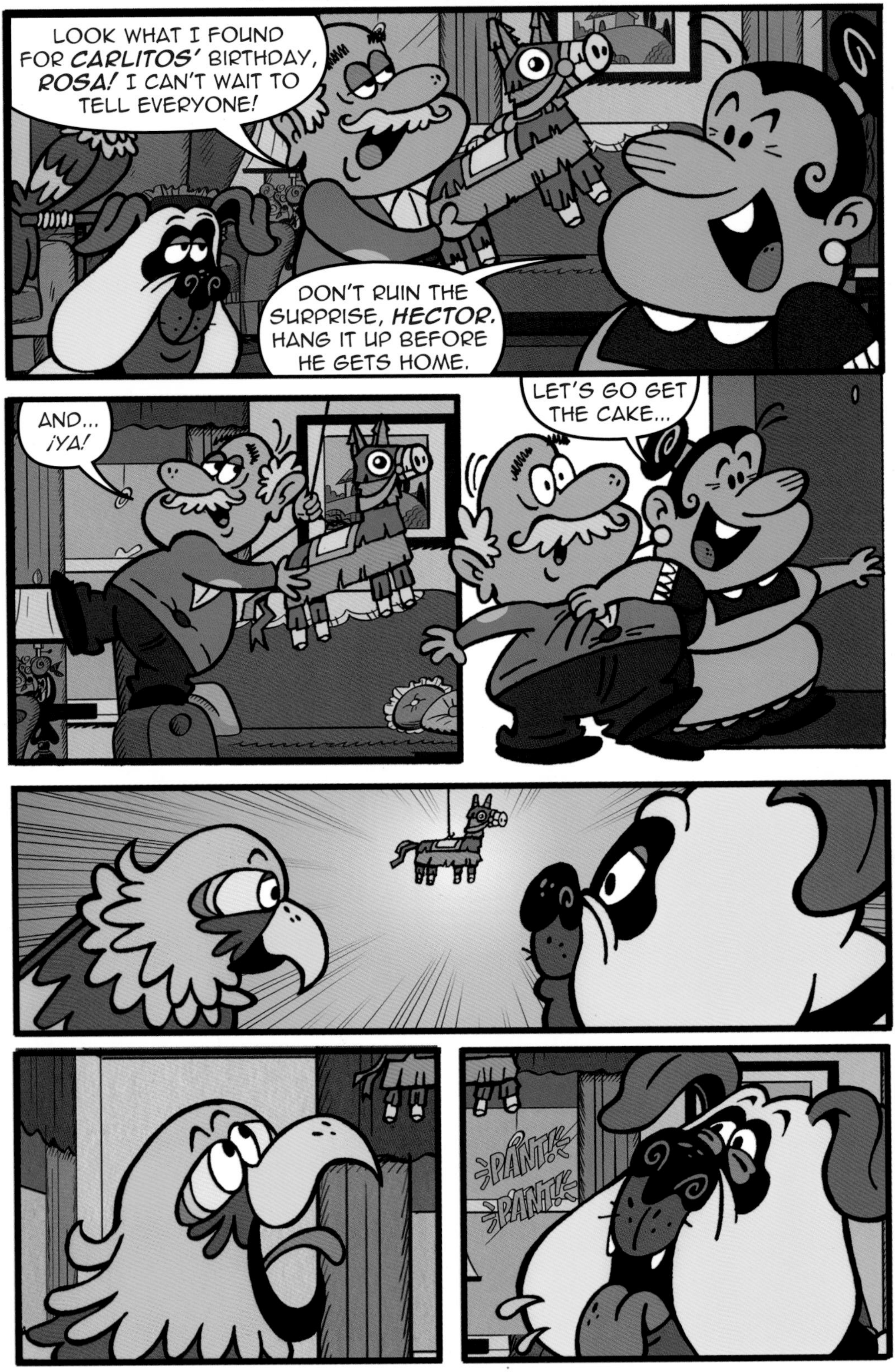
LOOK WHAT I FOUND FOR CARLITOS' BIRTHDAY, ROSA! I CAN'T WAIT TO TELL EVERYONE!
DON'T RUIN THE SURPRISE, HECTOR. HANG IT UP BEFORE HE GETS HOME.
AND... ¡YA!
LET'S GO GET THE CAKE...
PANT! PANT!

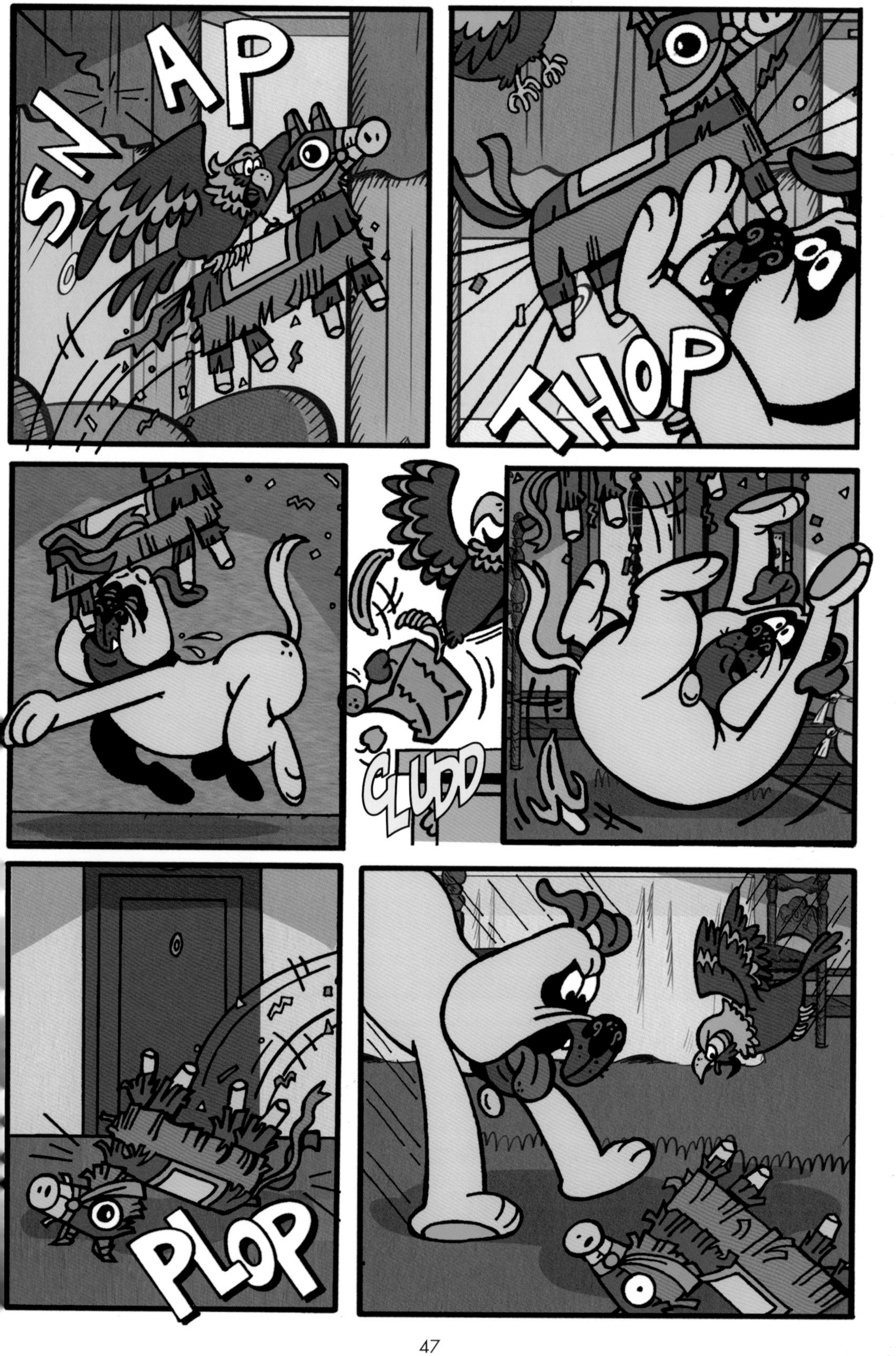
SNAP
THOP
CLUDD
PLOP

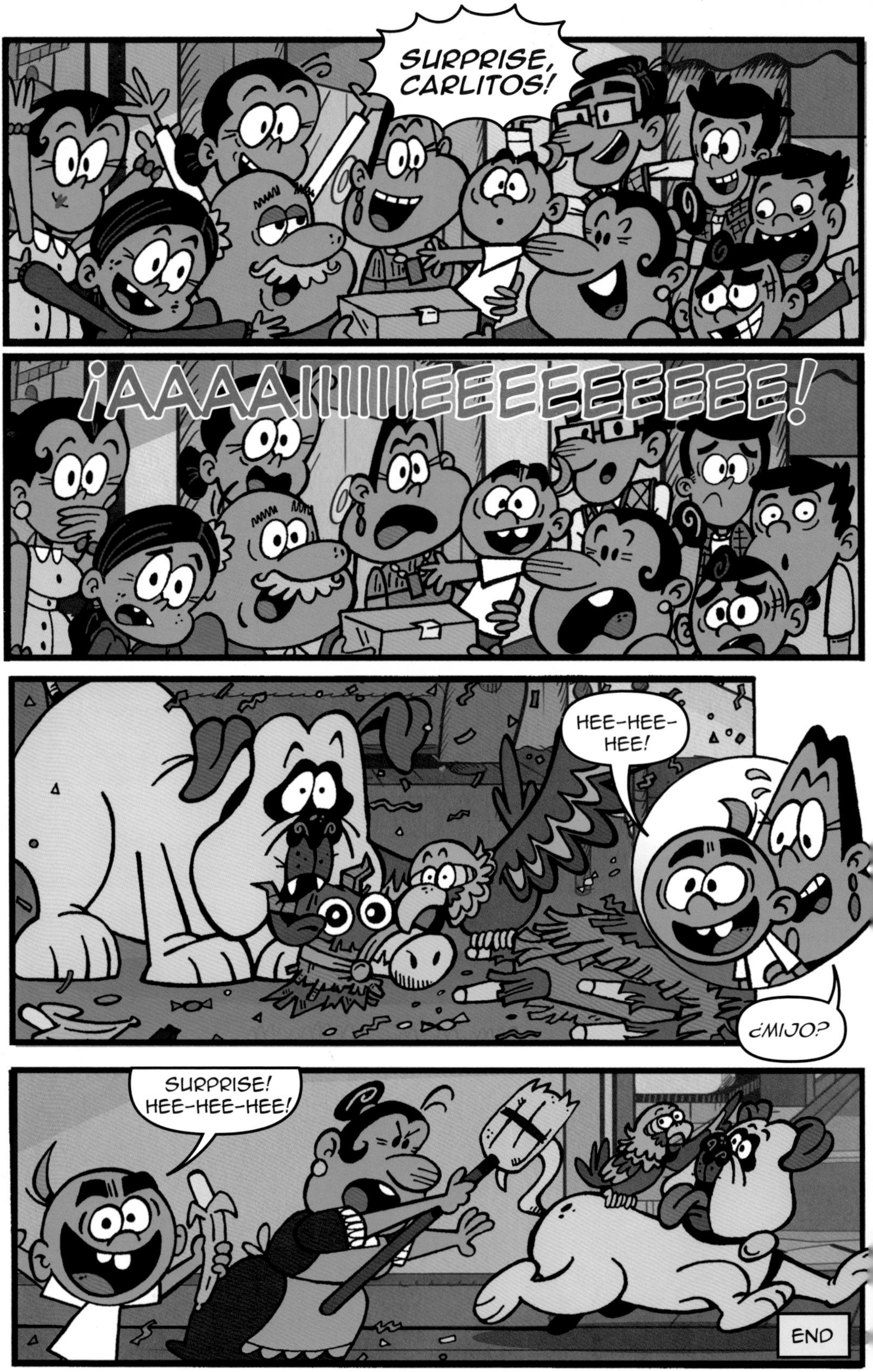
SURPRISE, CARLITOS!
¡AAAAIIIIIIEEEEEEEEEE!
HEE-HEE-HEE!
¿MIJO?
SURPRISE! HEE-HEE-HEE!
END

"GOSSIP GUY"

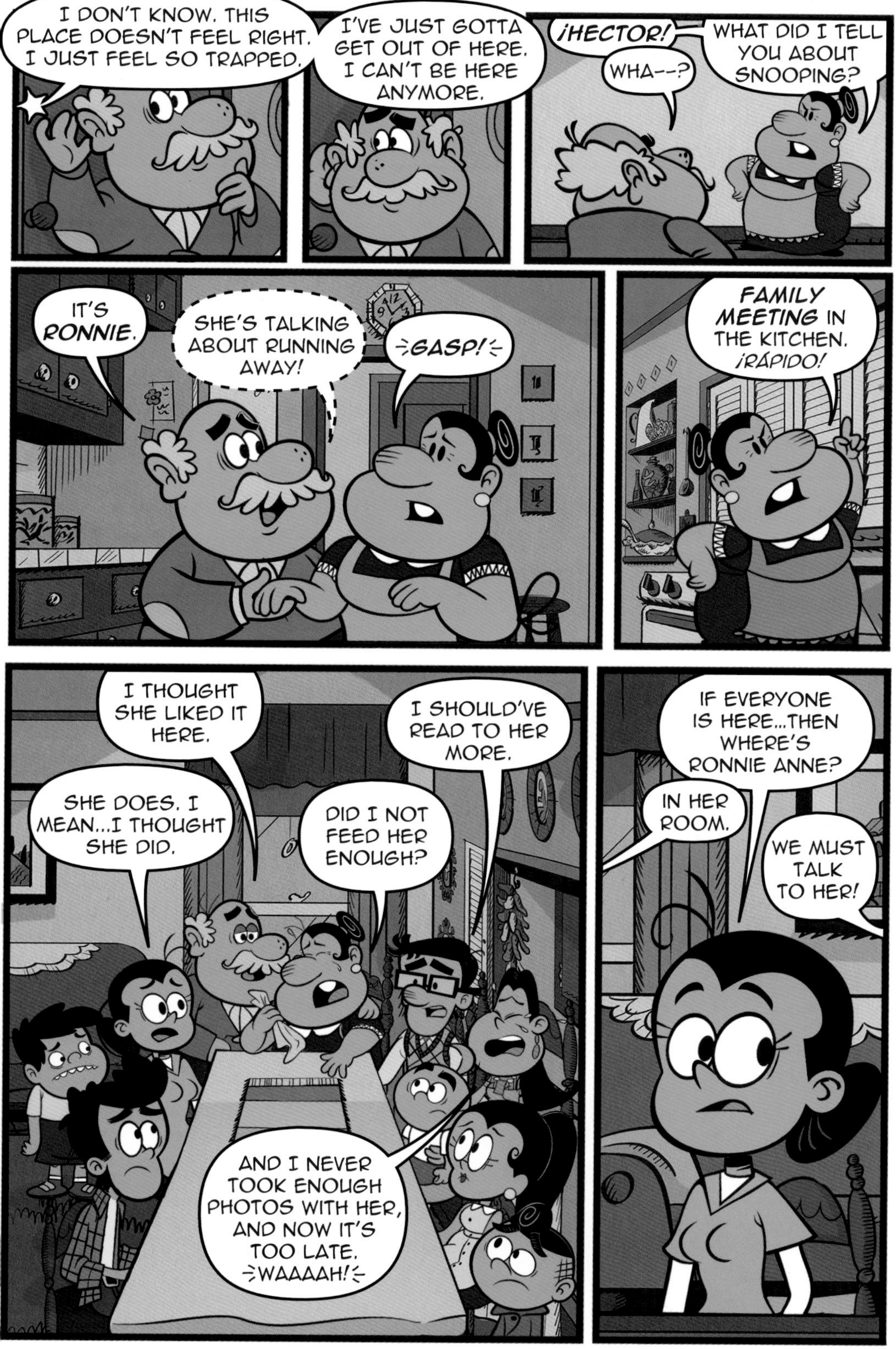

I DON'T KNOW. THIS PLACE DOESN'T FEEL RIGHT. I JUST FEEL SO TRAPPED.
I'VE JUST GOTTA GET OUT OF HERE. I CAN'T BE HERE ANYMORE.
¡HECTOR!
WHA--?
WHAT DID I TELL YOU ABOUT SNOOPING?
IT'S RONNIE.
SHE'S TALKING ABOUT RUNNING AWAY!
GASP!
FAMILY MEETING IN THE KITCHEN. ¡RÁPIDO!
I THOUGHT SHE LIKED IT HERE.
SHE DOES. I MEAN...I THOUGHT SHE DID.
I SHOULD'VE READ TO HER MORE.
DID I NOT FEED HER ENOUGH?
AND I NEVER TOOK ENOUGH PHOTOS WITH HER, AND NOW IT'S TOO LATE. WAAAAH!
IF EVERYONE IS HERE...THEN WHERE'S RONNIE ANNE?
IN HER ROOM.
WE MUST TALK TO HER!

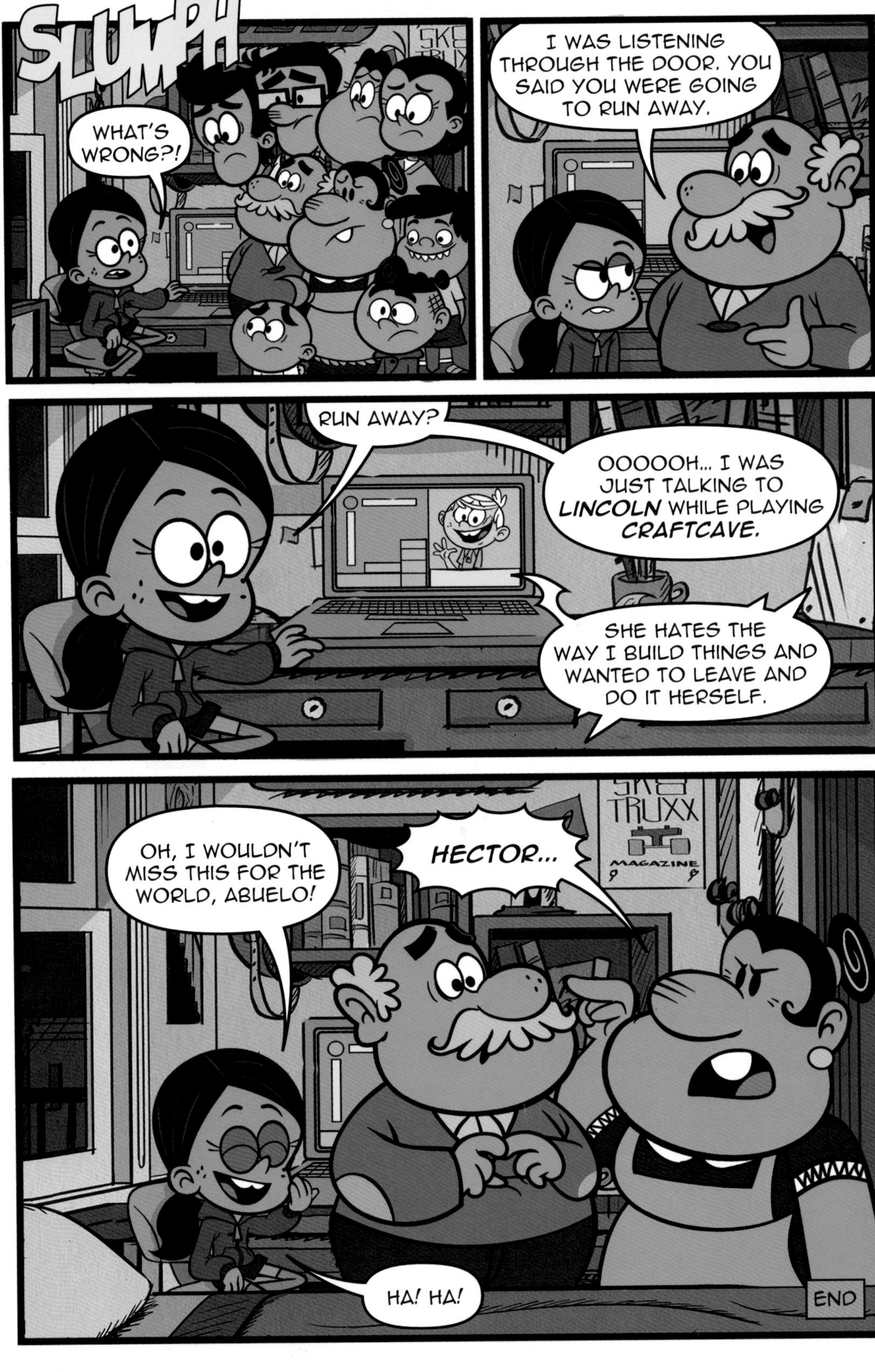

SLUMPH
WHAT'S WRONG?!
I WAS LISTENING THROUGH THE DOOR. YOU SAID YOU WERE GOING TO RUN AWAY.
RUN AWAY?
OOOOOH... I WAS JUST TALKING TO LINCOLN WHILE PLAYING CRAFTCAVE.
SHE HATES THE WAY I BUILD THINGS AND WANTED TO LEAVE AND DO IT HERSELF.
SK8 TRUXX
MAGAZINE
OH, I WOULDN'T MISS THIS FOR THE WORLD, ABUELO!
HECTOR...
HA! HA!
END

"WASHED UP"

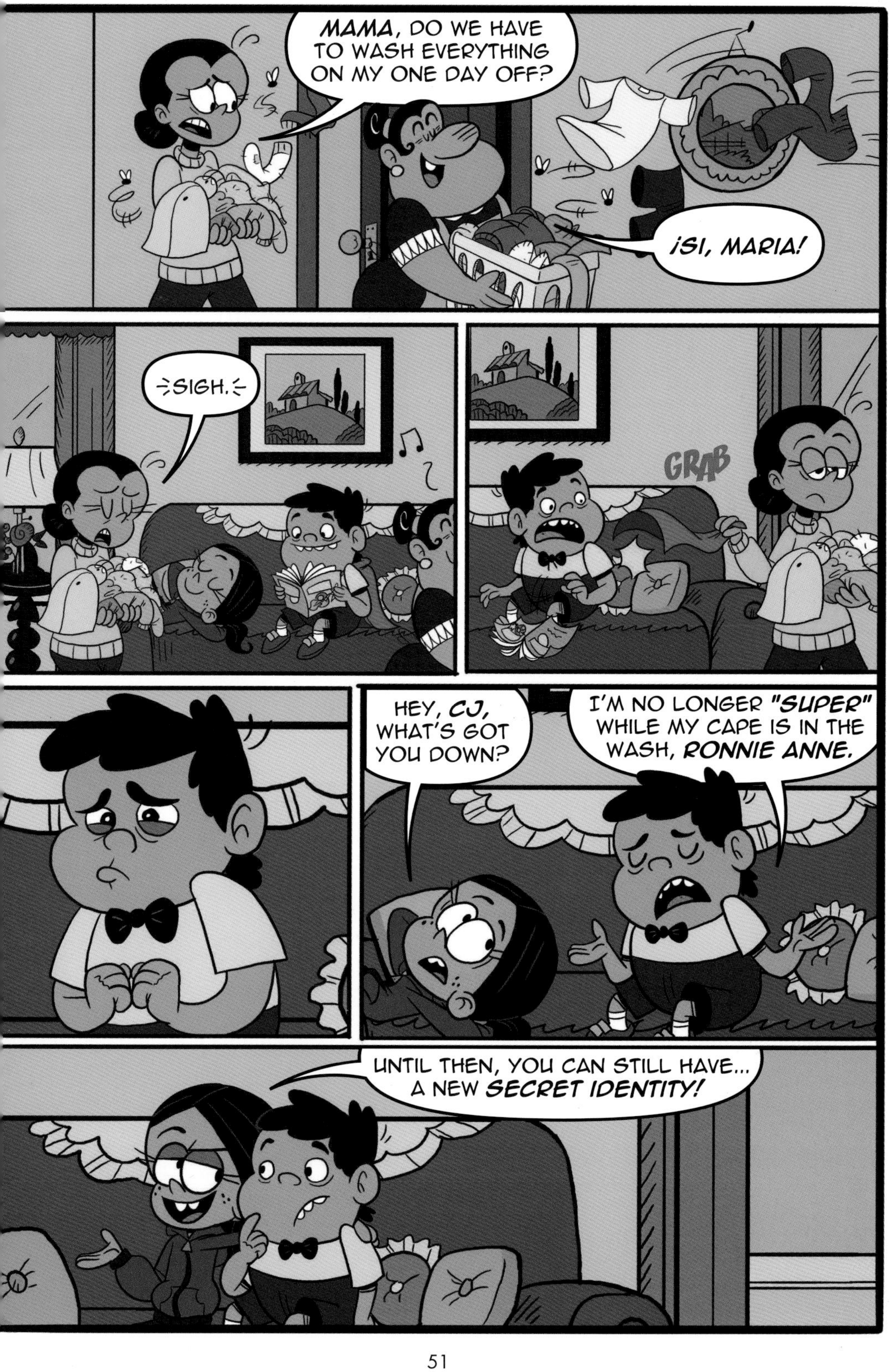
MAMA, DO WE HAVE TO WASH EVERYTHING ON MY ONE DAY OFF?
¡SI, MARIA!
SIGH.
GRAB
HEY, CJ, WHAT'S GOT YOU DOWN?
I'M NO LONGER "SUPER" WHILE MY CAPE IS IN THE WASH, RONNIE ANNE.
UNTIL THEN, YOU CAN STILL HAVE... A NEW SECRET IDENTITY!

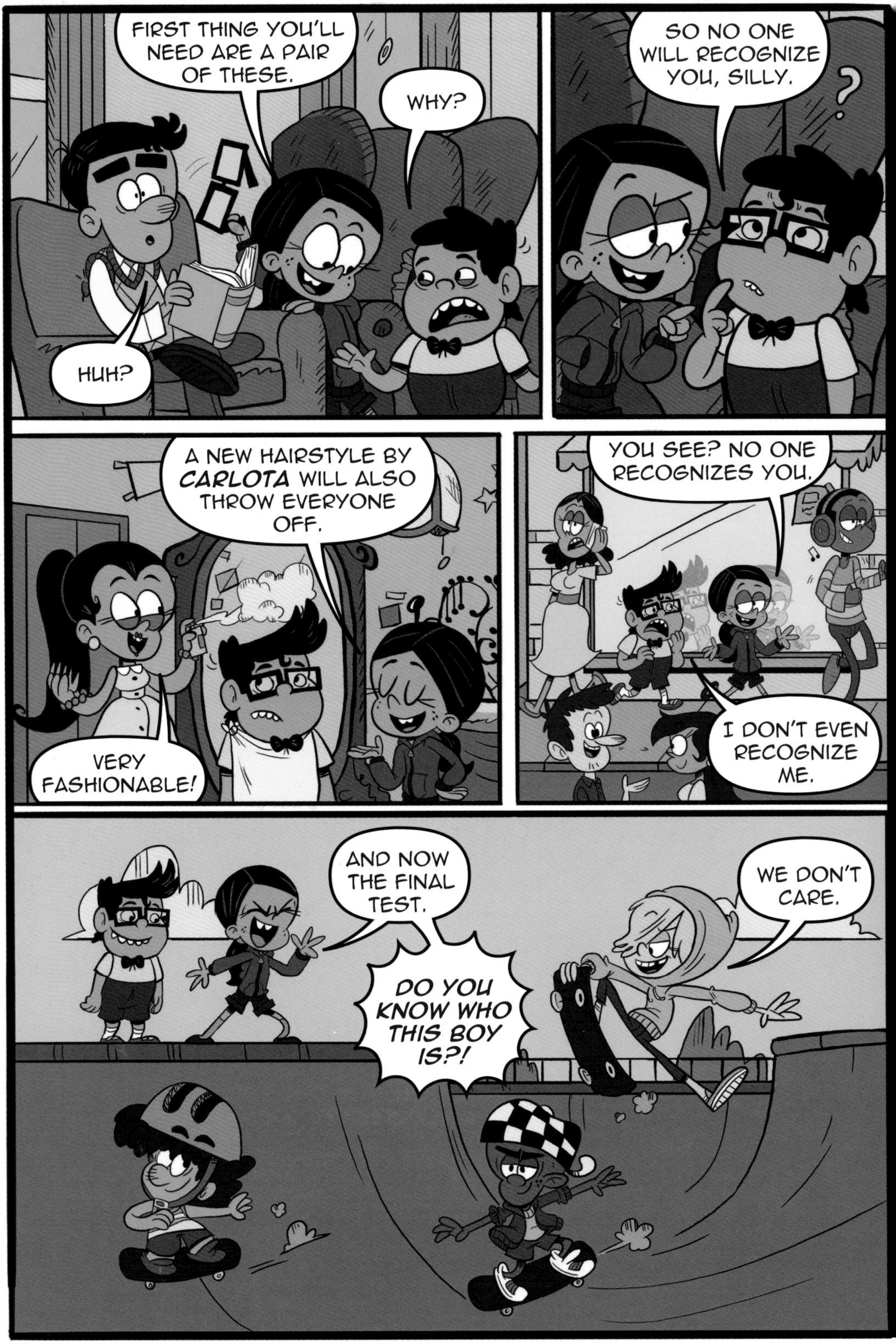
FIRST THING YOU'LL NEED ARE A PAIR OF THESE.
HUH?
WHY?
SO NO ONE WILL RECOGNIZE YOU, SILLY.
?
A NEW HAIRSTYLE BY *CARLOTA* WILL ALSO THROW EVERYONE OFF.
VERY FASHIONABLE!
YOU SEE? NO ONE RECOGNIZES YOU.
I DON'T EVEN RECOGNIZE ME.
AND NOW THE FINAL TEST.
DO YOU KNOW WHO THIS BOY IS?!
WE DON'T CARE.

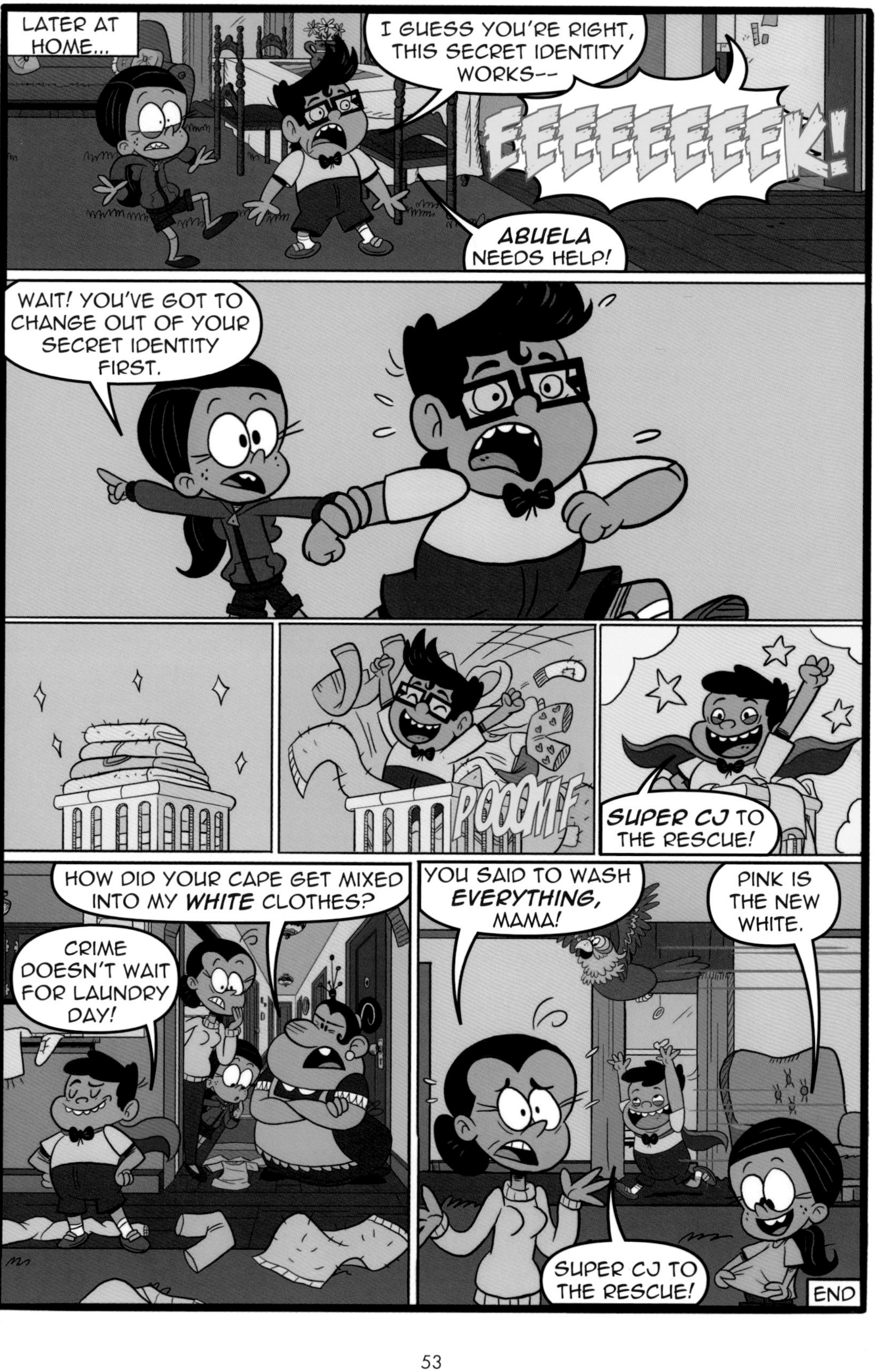

LATER AT HOME...
I GUESS YOU'RE RIGHT, THIS SECRET IDENTITY WORKS--
EEEEEEEEEK!
ABUELA NEEDS HELP!
WAIT! YOU'VE GOT TO CHANGE OUT OF YOUR SECRET IDENTITY FIRST.
POOOMF
SUPER CJ TO THE RESCUE!
HOW DID YOUR CAPE GET MIXED INTO MY WHITE CLOTHES?
CRIME DOESN'T WAIT FOR LAUNDRY DAY!
YOU SAID TO WASH EVERYTHING, MAMA!
PINK IS THE NEW WHITE.
SUPER CJ TO THE RESCUE!
END

"LIFE IMITATES ART"

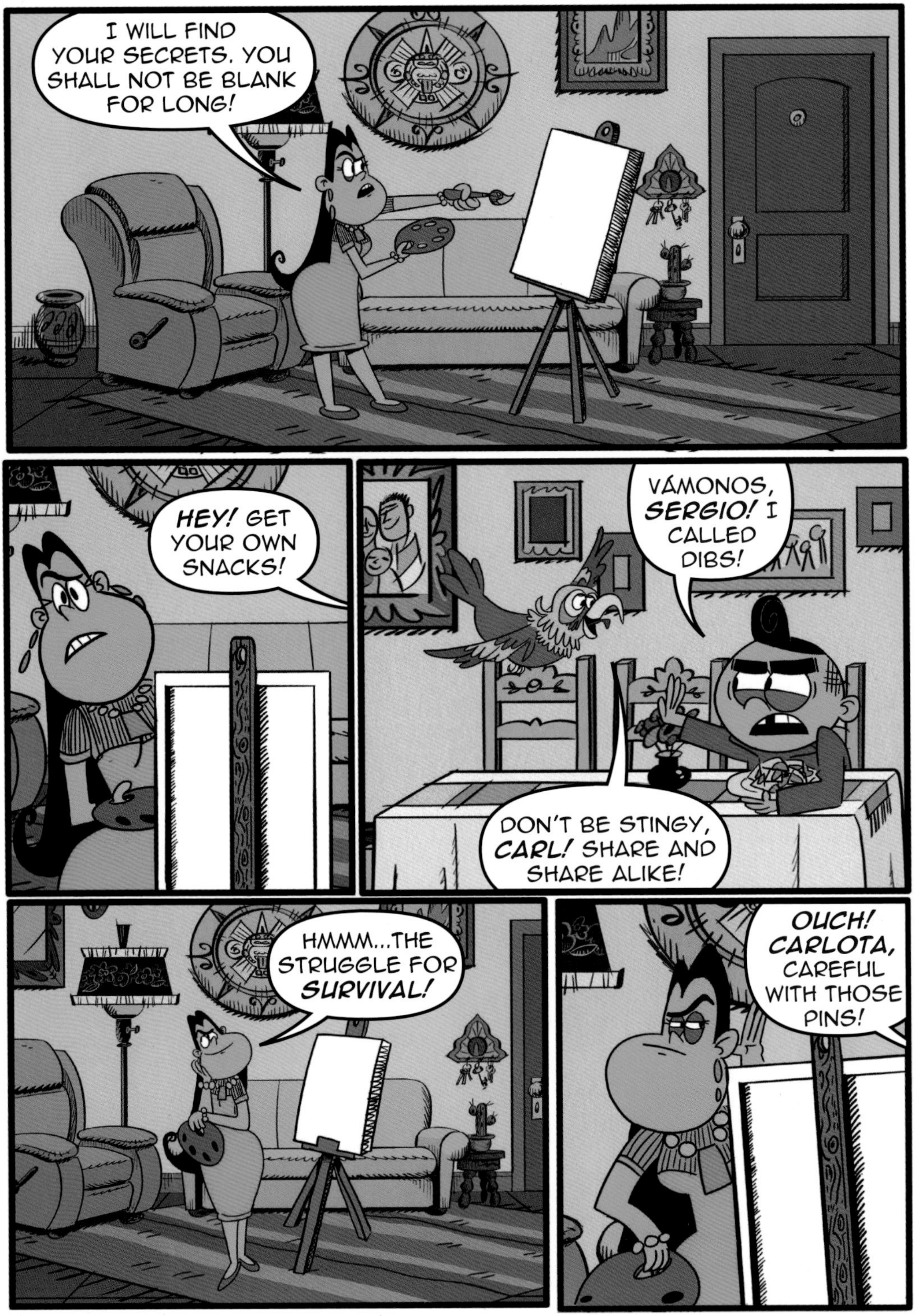

I WILL FIND YOUR SECRETS. YOU SHALL NOT BE BLANK FOR LONG!
HEY! GET YOUR OWN SNACKS!
VÁMONOS, SERGIO! I CALLED DIBS!
DON'T BE STINGY, CARL! SHARE AND SHARE ALIKE!
HMMM...THE STRUGGLE FOR SURVIVAL!
OUCH! CARLOTA, CAREFUL WITH THOSE PINS!

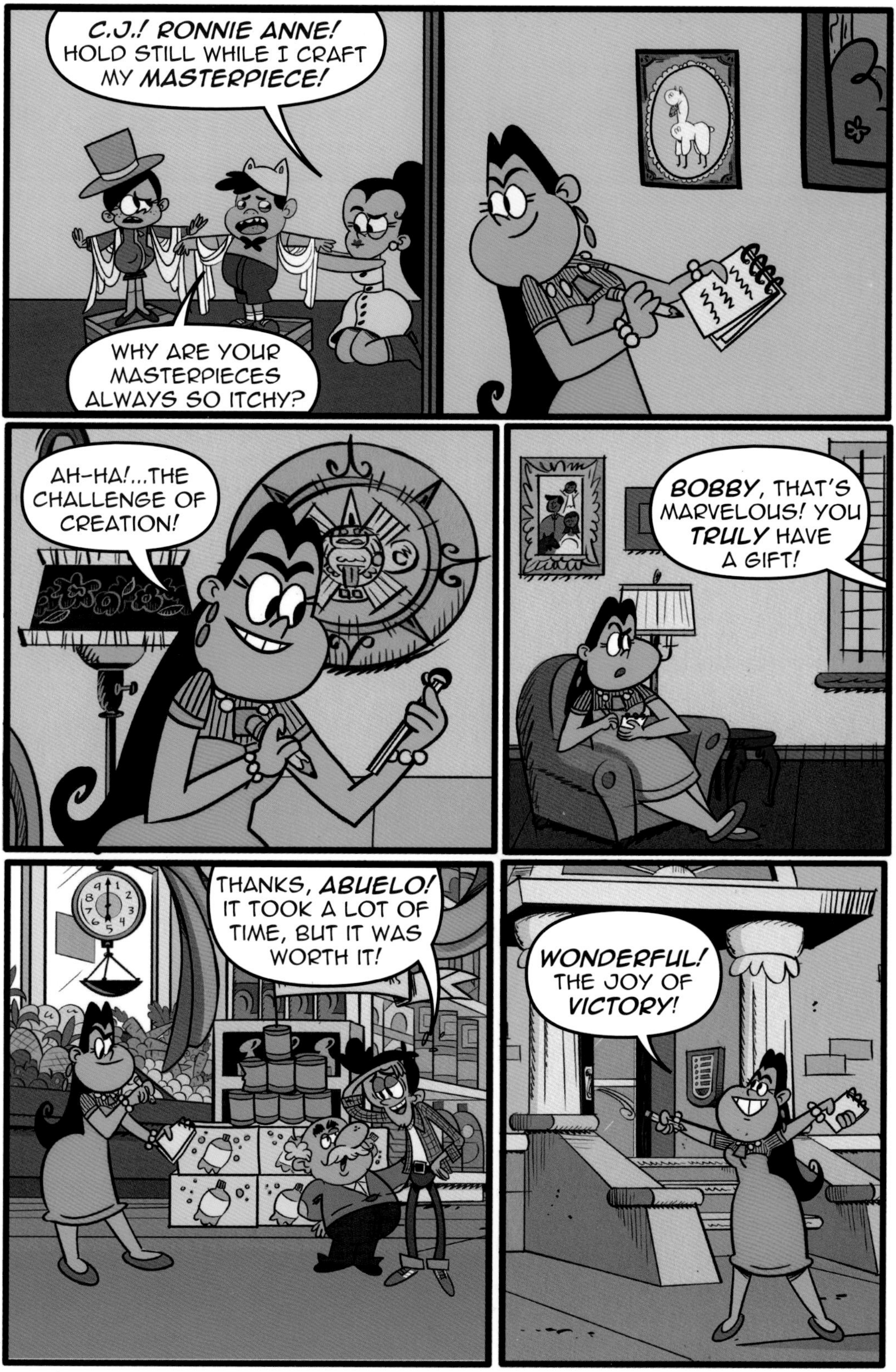
C.J.! RONNIE ANNE! HOLD STILL WHILE I CRAFT MY MASTERPIECE!
WHY ARE YOUR MASTERPIECES ALWAYS SO ITCHY?
AH-HA!...THE CHALLENGE OF CREATION!
BOBBY, THAT'S MARVELOUS! YOU TRULY HAVE A GIFT!
THANKS, ABUELO! IT TOOK A LOT OF TIME, BUT IT WAS WORTH IT!
WONDERFUL! THE JOY OF VICTORY!

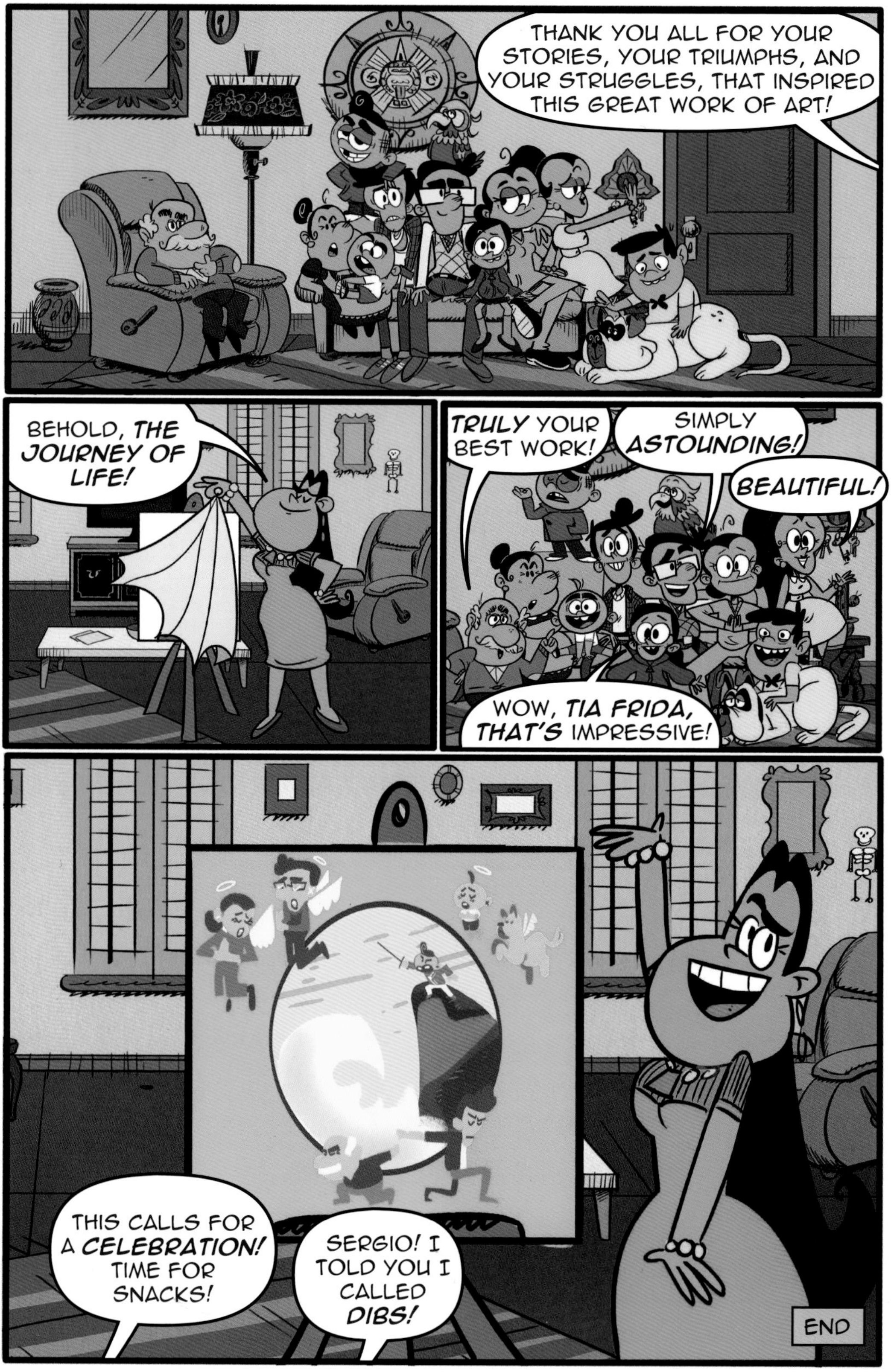

THANK YOU ALL FOR YOUR STORIES, YOUR TRIUMPHS, AND YOUR STRUGGLES, THAT INSPIRED THIS GREAT WORK OF ART!
BEHOLD, *THE JOURNEY OF LIFE!*
TRULY YOUR BEST WORK!
SIMPLY *ASTOUNDING!*
BEAUTIFUL!
WOW, *TIA FRIDA, THAT'S* IMPRESSIVE!
THIS CALLS FOR A *CELEBRATION!* TIME FOR SNACKS!
SERGIO! I TOLD YOU I CALLED *DIBS!*
END

"THE GREAT ESCAPE"

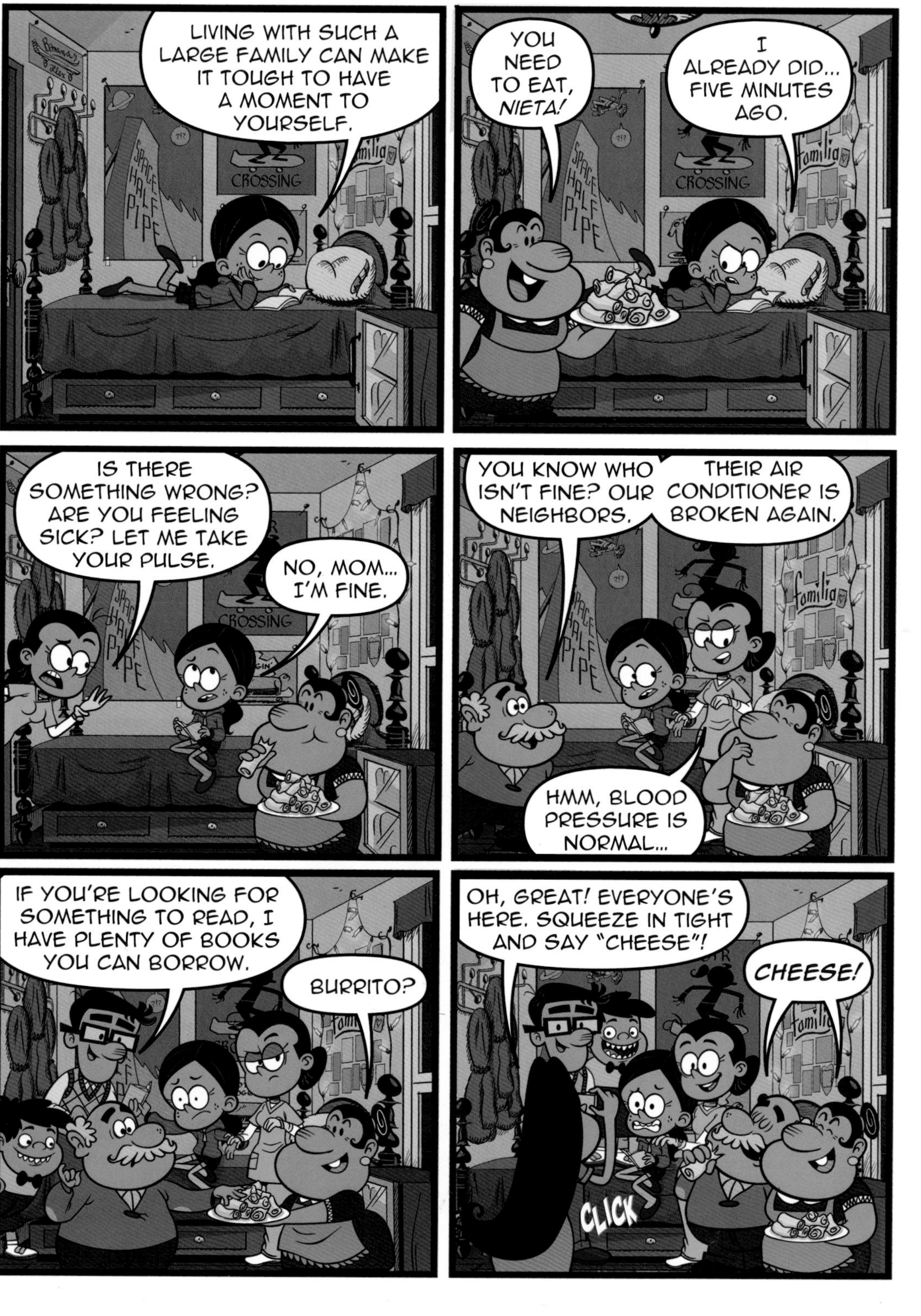
LIVING WITH SUCH A LARGE FAMILY CAN MAKE IT TOUGH TO HAVE A MOMENT TO YOURSELF.
SPACE HALF PIPE
CROSSING
familia
YOU NEED TO EAT, NIETA!
I ALREADY DID... FIVE MINUTES AGO.
IS THERE SOMETHING WRONG? ARE YOU FEELING SICK? LET ME TAKE YOUR PULSE.
NO, MOM... I'M FINE.
YOU KNOW WHO ISN'T FINE? OUR NEIGHBORS.
THEIR AIR CONDITIONER IS BROKEN AGAIN.
HMM, BLOOD PRESSURE IS NORMAL...
IF YOU'RE LOOKING FOR SOMETHING TO READ, I HAVE PLENTY OF BOOKS YOU CAN BORROW.
BURRITO?
OH, GREAT! EVERYONE'S HERE. SQUEEZE IN TIGHT AND SAY "CHEESE"!
CHEESE!
CLICK

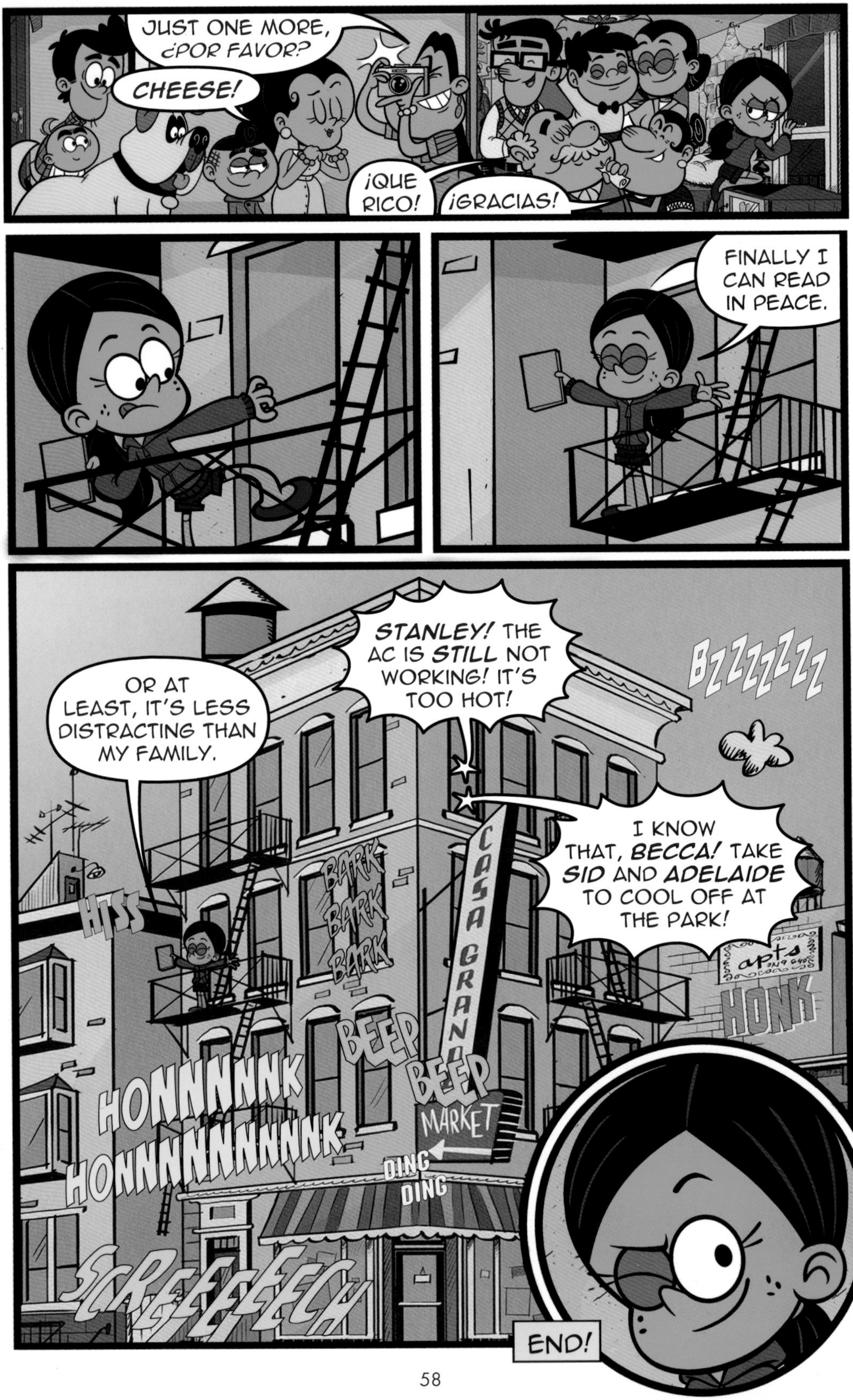
JUST ONE MORE, ¿POR FAVOR?
CHEESE!
¡QUE RICO!
¡GRACIAS!
FINALLY I CAN READ IN PEACE.
OR AT LEAST, IT'S LESS DISTRACTING THAN MY FAMILY.
STANLEY! THE AC IS STILL NOT WORKING! IT'S TOO HOT!
BZZZZZZZ
I KNOW THAT, BECCA! TAKE SID AND ADELAIDE TO COOL OFF AT THE PARK!
CASA GRANDE
BARK
BARK
BARK
HISS
HONK
BEEP
BEEP
HONNNNNK
HONNNNNNNNNK
MARKET
DING
DING
SCREEEEECH
END!

"THE MASKED MAN"

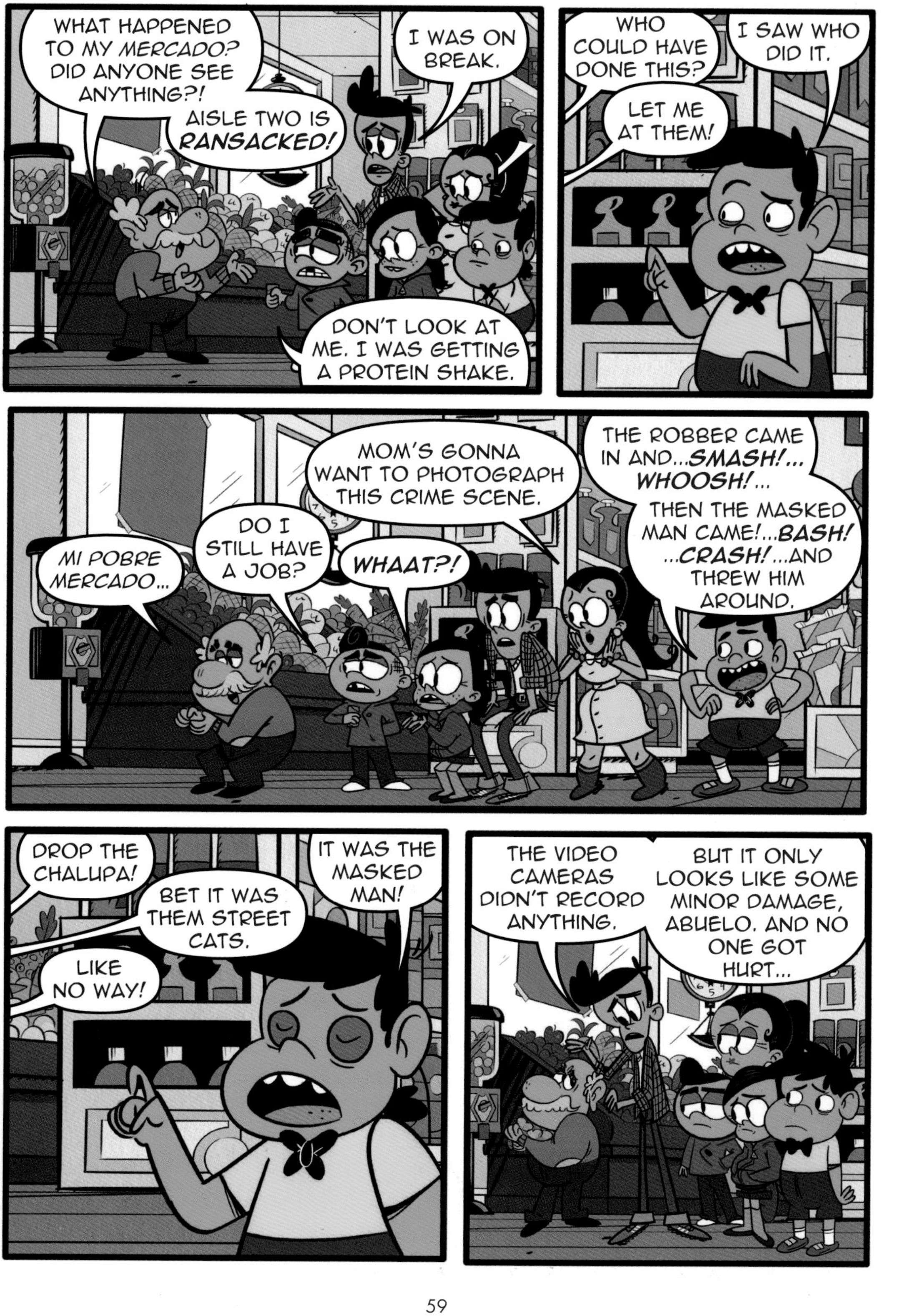
WHAT HAPPENED TO MY *MERCADO*? DID ANYONE SEE ANYTHING?!
AISLE TWO IS ***RANSACKED!***
I WAS ON BREAK.
DON'T LOOK AT ME. I WAS GETTING A PROTEIN SHAKE.
WHO COULD HAVE DONE THIS?
LET ME AT THEM!
I SAW WHO DID IT.
MI POBRE MERCADO...
DO I STILL HAVE A JOB?
WHAAT?!
MOM'S GONNA WANT TO PHOTOGRAPH THIS CRIME SCENE.
THE ROBBER CAME IN AND...***SMASH!***...***WHOOSH!***...
THEN THE MASKED MAN CAME!...***BASH!*** ...***CRASH!***...AND THREW HIM AROUND.
DROP THE CHALUPA!
BET IT WAS THEM STREET CATS.
LIKE NO WAY!
IT WAS THE MASKED MAN!
THE VIDEO CAMERAS DIDN'T RECORD ANYTHING.
BUT IT ONLY LOOKS LIKE SOME MINOR DAMAGE, ABUELO. AND NO ONE GOT HURT...

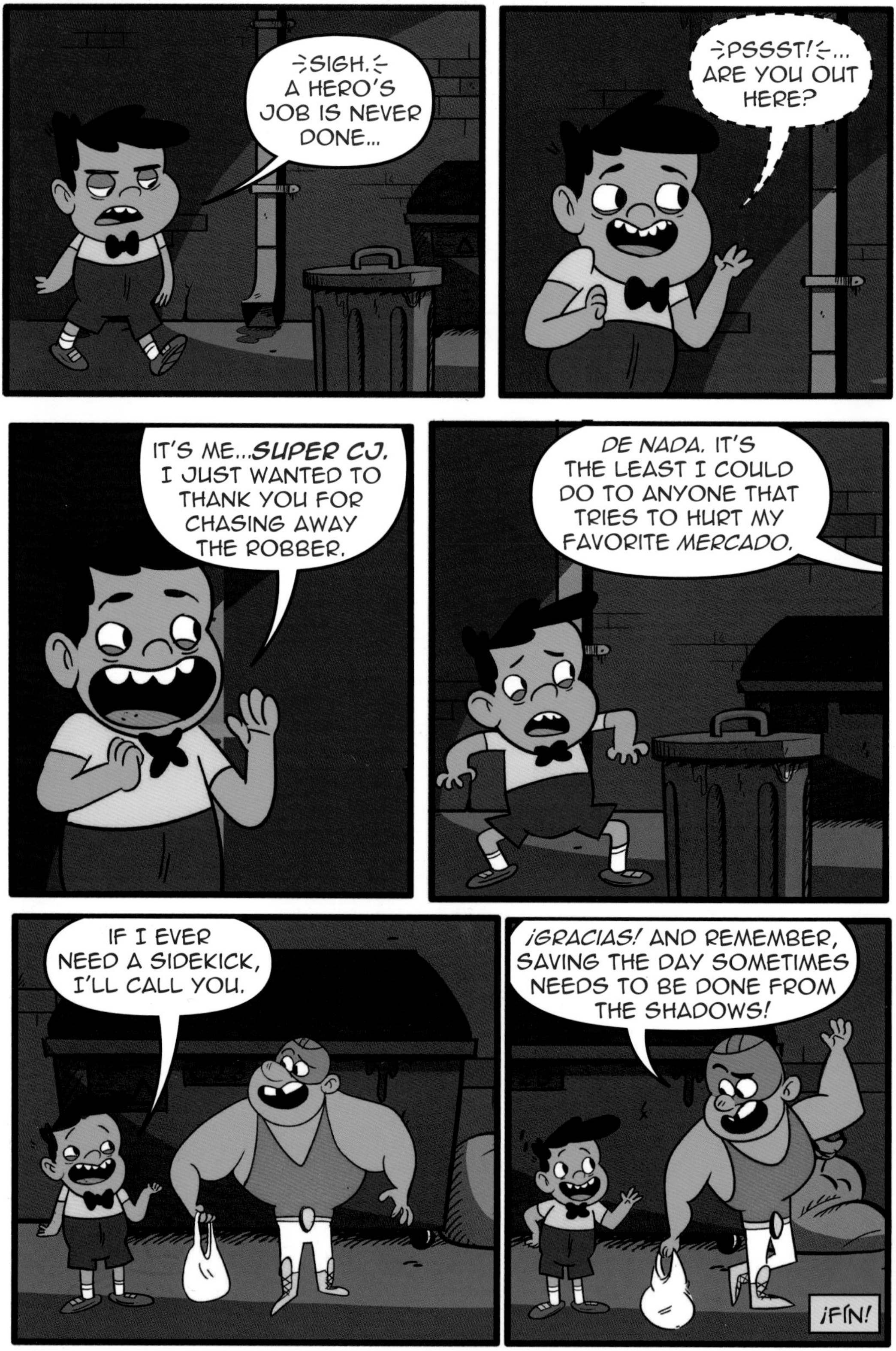

SIGH.
A HERO'S JOB IS NEVER DONE...
PSSST!... ARE YOU OUT HERE?
IT'S ME...**SUPER CJ.** I JUST WANTED TO THANK YOU FOR CHASING AWAY THE ROBBER.
DE NADA. IT'S THE LEAST I COULD DO TO ANYONE THAT TRIES TO HURT MY FAVORITE *MERCADO.*
IF I EVER NEED A SIDEKICK, I'LL CALL YOU.
¡GRACIAS! AND REMEMBER, SAVING THE DAY SOMETIMES NEEDS TO BE DONE FROM THE SHADOWS!
¡FIN!

"MY BOBBY AND ME"

GOOD MORNING, **BOBBY!** HAVE A GREAT DAY AT THE MERCADO.

ACTUALLY, I TOOK THE DAY OFF, **RONNIE ANNE.** WANTED TO SPEND SOME QUALITY TIME WITH MY FAVORITE LITTLE SISTER.

BOBBY, THAT'S SO **COOL!** YOU **NEVER** TAKE SATURDAY OFF.

FIGURED WE SHOULD EXPLORE THIS AMAZING CITY TOGETHER, **NINI.** I'VE GOT THE WHOLE DAY PLANNED!

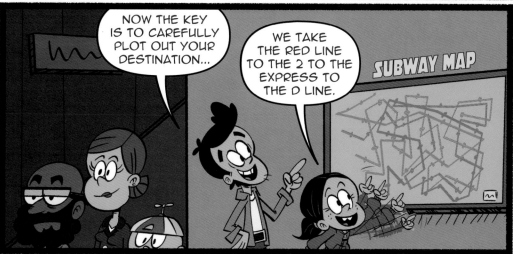

NOW THE KEY IS TO CAREFULLY PLOT OUT YOUR DESTINATION...

WE TAKE THE RED LINE TO THE 2 TO THE EXPRESS TO THE D LINE.

SUBWAY MAP

SO THE CITY PARK IS MY ALL-TIME FAVORITE PLACE TO UNWIND. YOU CAN FEED THE DUCKS, PLAY CHECKERS--

QUACK QUACK

AND **SHRED!** COME ON, BOBBY! I'LL SHOW YOU THE HALF PIPE.

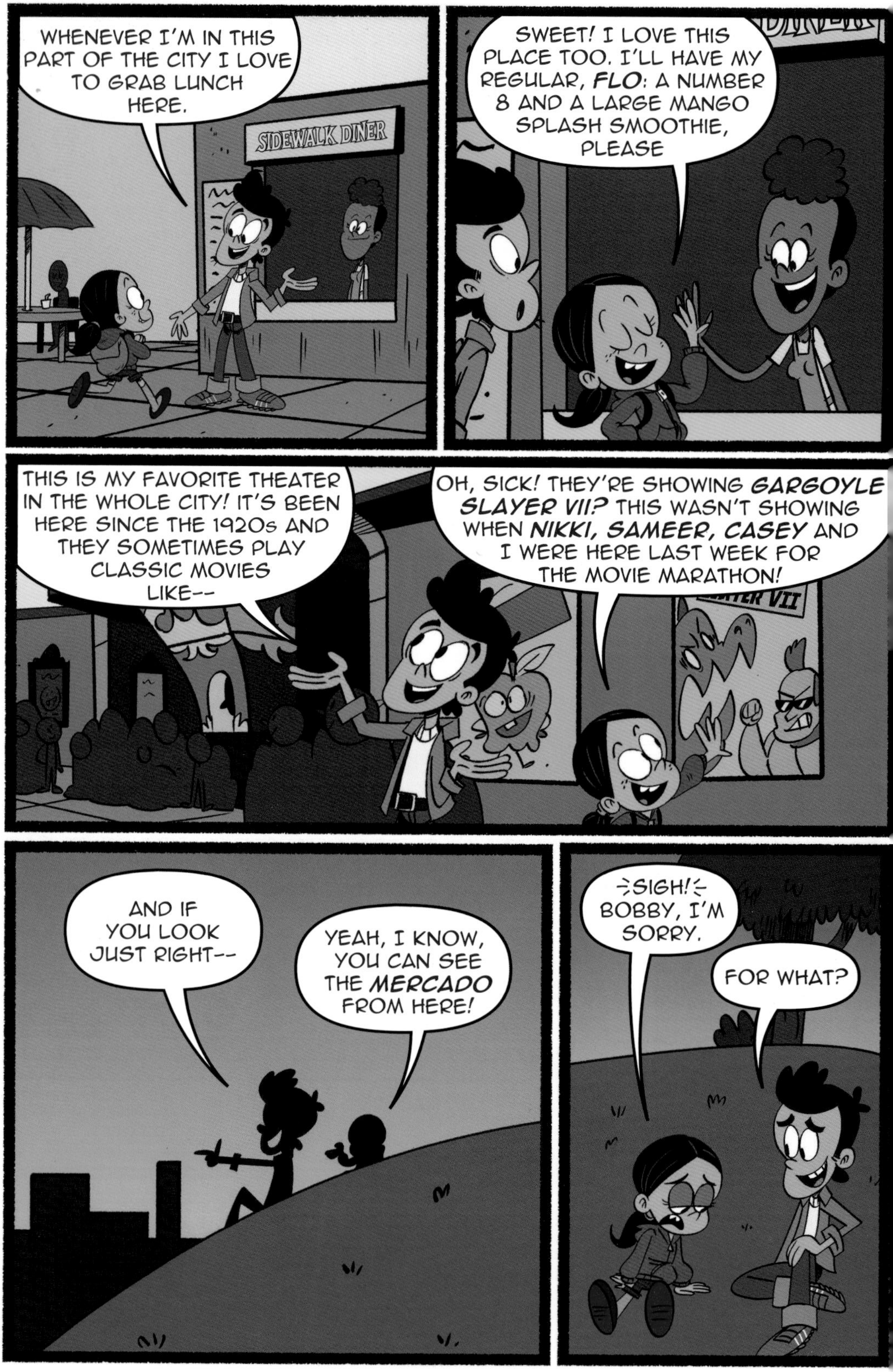
WHENEVER I'M IN THIS PART OF THE CITY I LOVE TO GRAB LUNCH HERE.
SIDEWALK DINER
SWEET! I LOVE THIS PLACE TOO. I'LL HAVE MY REGULAR, FLO: A NUMBER 8 AND A LARGE MANGO SPLASH SMOOTHIE, PLEASE
THIS IS MY FAVORITE THEATER IN THE WHOLE CITY! IT'S BEEN HERE SINCE THE 1920s AND THEY SOMETIMES PLAY CLASSIC MOVIES LIKE--
OH, SICK! THEY'RE SHOWING GARGOYLE SLAYER VII? THIS WASN'T SHOWING WHEN NIKKI, SAMEER, CASEY AND I WERE HERE LAST WEEK FOR THE MOVIE MARATHON!
AND IF YOU LOOK JUST RIGHT--
YEAH, I KNOW, YOU CAN SEE THE MERCADO FROM HERE!
SIGH! BOBBY, I'M SORRY.
FOR WHAT?

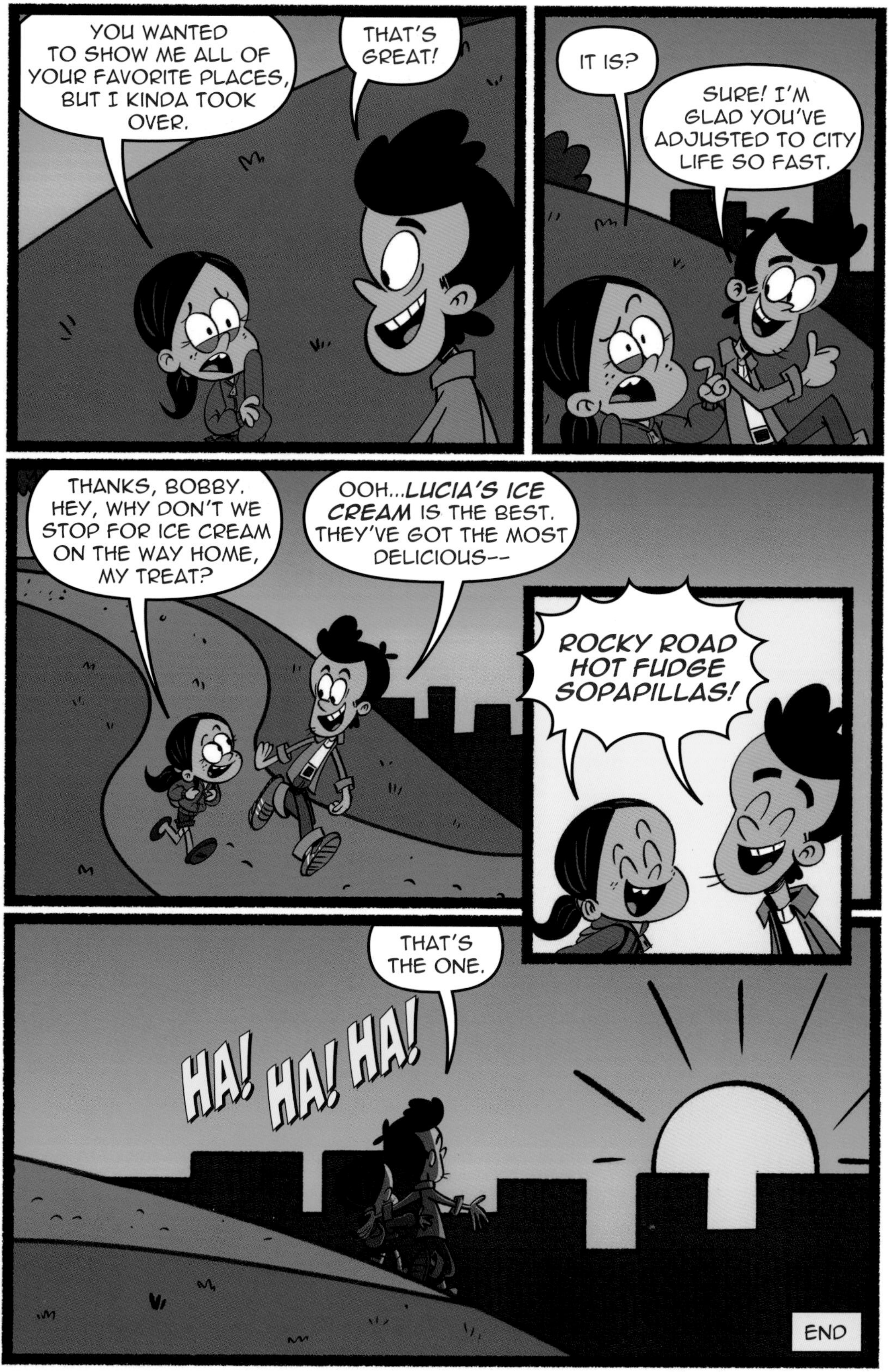
YOU WANTED TO SHOW ME ALL OF YOUR FAVORITE PLACES, BUT I KINDA TOOK OVER.
THAT'S GREAT!
IT IS?
SURE! I'M GLAD YOU'VE ADJUSTED TO CITY LIFE SO FAST.
THANKS, BOBBY. HEY, WHY DON'T WE STOP FOR ICE CREAM ON THE WAY HOME, MY TREAT?
OOH...*LUCIA'S ICE CREAM* IS THE BEST. THEY'VE GOT THE MOST DELICIOUS--
ROCKY ROAD HOT FUDGE SOPAPILLAS!
THAT'S THE ONE.
HA! HA! HA!
END

WATCH OUT FOR PAPERCUTZ™

Welcome to the entertaining eighth THE LOUD HOUSE graphic novel, "Livin' La Casa Loud," from Papercutz – those comics-loving gringos dedicated to publishing great graphic novels for all ages. *Hola!* I'm Jim Salicrup, Editor-in-Chief and Erstwhile Bronx *Mercado* Frequenter, and I'm here to offer up a few recommendations for other graphic novel series you may also enjoy… But first, I want to thank you for picking up THE LOUD HOUSE #8. Whether you got this graphic novel either digitally or in print, as a gift, bought it yourself, or borrowed it from a friend or library, we thank you. Why? Because your support makes it possible for us to create even more graphic novels featuring THE LOUD HOUSE. Just like THE LOUD HOUSE has grown to be a super success on Nickelodeon, THE LOUD HOUSE graphic novels are becoming more and more popular every day thanks to fans like you.

We realize you're probably busy, between watching THE LOUD HOUSE on Nickelodeon and collecting the graphic novels, not to mention all the other stuff you're doing… but if you're really enjoying THE LOUD HOUSE graphic novels, and wondering if there might be other Papercutz graphic novels you might enjoy too, well, you're in luck, as I'm happy to mention a few!

REDCODE · ALBBIE · AIR TEAM
DINOSAUR EXPLORERS
LOST IN THE JURASSIC
PAPERCUTZ

©2019 Kadokawa Gempak Starz.

DINOSAUR EXPLORERS – Imagine being flung back in time to the days when dinosaurs walked the earth. Well, that's exactly what happened to Sean, Stone, Rain, and Emily. They, along with scientists Dr. Da Vinci and Diana, are now jumping back through time to the present, but at only so many centuries at a time. As a result, they're able to explore and encounter creatures no man has ever seen alive and in their natural habitat. That may be great for scientific research, but not so good if the dinosaurs happen to be really hungry…

Cazenove
William
The Sisters
3 Honestly, I Love My Sister
PAPERCUTZ

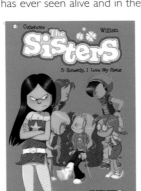

© 2019 BAMBOO ÉDITION.

THE SISTERS – Wendy and her younger sister Maureen love each other, but that doesn't mean they get along perfectly. They're always doing something that will in some way, somehow upset each other. It might be Maureen stealing peeks into Wendy's private diary, or simply misunderstanding what her sister tells her. It's not all bad – Wendy and Maureen also imagine themselves as superheroes fighting side-by-side. No matter what, stuff happens. And it's usually very funny.

Lucy & Liz Lareau Ryan Jampole
Suzannah Rowntree & Scott Couto
geeky f@b 5
DOGgone CATastrophe
PAPERCUTZ

©2019 by Geeky Fab Five, Inc.

THE GEEKY F@B 5 – Animal lover Lucy, and her aspiring astronaut sister Marina, have moved to the town of Normal, Illinois, where they have joined three friends from school – math whiz and singer Zara, robotics engineer A.J., and computer coder and fashionista Sofia – to form The Geeky F@b 5. Oh, and their unofficial mascot, Hubble the snarky cat, usually helps out or complicates matters, depending on his unique point of view. Together the girls are able to combine their talents to solve all sorts of problems, because when girls stick together, anything is possible.

While we hope you check out these Papercutz graphic novels, we're sure you won't want to miss THE LOUD HOUSE #9 "Ultimate Hangout" – coming soon! Find out what happens when Lincoln and his friends have the run of the house when his sisters are away for the day…

Gracias,

Jim

STAY IN TOUCH!

EMAIL:	salicrup@papercutz.com
WEB:	papercutz.com
TWITTER:	@papercutzgn
INSTAGRAM:	@papercutzgn
FACEBOOK:	PAPERCUTZGRAPHICNOVELS
FANMAIL:	Papercutz, 160 Broadway, Suite 700, East Wing, New York, NY 10038